Contents

The Princess and the Plumber *3*

Mermaid in the Jar *11*

The Miss and Sylvia and Sam *13*

The Woman Who Lived in a Shoe *21*

The Middleman to Elda *25*

The Fundamental Race *29*

The Littlest Dumpling *33*

The Favourite Monkey *37*

The Giant *43*

The Girl Who Was Blind All the Time *47*

The Moon Monologue *51*

The Party at Her Place, with Her Piano *55*

The Girl Who Planted Flowers *59*

Eleanor *63*

The Accident *71*

Mr. Jones's First Outing *73*

A Few Adventures of the Young Fornicator *79*

What Changed *83*

Janis and Marcus *89*

The Raspberry Bush *93*

Frames from Christianity *95*

A Bench for Marianne and Todd *99*

The Poet and the Novelist as Roommates *103*

The Sort of Woman Freeman Loved *109*

The Night of Rory *115*

The Man from Out of Town *119*

The Little Old Lady and the Little Old Man *125*

The House at the End of the Lane *129*

Cows and Bread *133*

The Man with the Hat *135*

Notes *143*

For my family

THE MIDDLE STORIES

SHEILA HETI

ANANSI

First published in hardcover in 2001 by House of Anansi Press Ltd.
This edition published in 2002 by
House of Anansi Press Inc.
110 Spadina Ave., Suite 801
Toronto, ON, M5V 2K4
Tel. 416-363-4343
Fax 416-363-1017
www.anansi.ca

Distributed in Canada by
Publishers Group Canada
250A Carlton Street
Toronto, ON, M5A 2L1
Tel. 416-934-9900
Toll free order numbers:
Tel. 800-663-5714
Fax 800-565-3770

05 04 03 02   1 2 3 4 5

Canadian Cataloguing in Publication Data

Heti, Sheila, 1976–
The middle stories

ISBN 0-88784-174-0(bound).
– ISBN 0-88784-677-7(pbk)
I. Title.

PS8565.E853M52 2001   C813'.6   C00-933190-5
PR9199.3.H47M52 2001

COVER AND BOOK DESIGN: BILL DOUGLAS AT THE BANG
FROG ILLUSTRATION: SHEILA HETI

THE CANADA COUNCIL | LE CONSEIL DES ARTS
FOR THE ARTS | DU CANADA
SINCE 1957 | DEPUIS 1957

We acknowledge for their financial support of our publishing program the Canada Council for the Arts, the Ontario
Arts Council, and the Government of Canada through the Book Publishing Industry Development Program (BPIDP).

Printed and bound in Canada

THE MIDDLE STORIES

THE MIDDLE STORIES

THE PRINCESS AND THE PLUMBER

A regional man who was just a plumber asked the princess to marry him. He was from the region so it was okay, partly, but he was a plumber, and knew that even if she loved him her father would say no.

She did not love him. She didn't even know him. When he went to present himself to her over the garden gate, she looked up from her book, over her sunglasses, and said, "Can't you see I'm a princess? I have no time for any common boys. I have no time for you. If you are a prince one day, then you can come and see me. Until then, I have no more words." Her legs were long and bare in the sun.

The plumber, being a modest fellow, was quite distressed. He was a good man, he thought, even a handsome man, and he deserved better than this.

"I'm strong," he said, "and I have a good sense of humour. You will see that if you will only spend one night with me. I can give you whatever you desire. I will make you very happy."

"I have said all I have to say and I'm not going to say any more," the princess replied. "I am not happy to talk to you." And she turned her head and picked up from the grass a sheet of metal tanning foil and blocked his view of her with it.

"All right for now," he said. "But I'm coming back."

That evening he went home and, using a hammer and some wood, built the most marvellous marriage contraption the world had ever seen. It takes a special kind of man to invent something new, something never before thought of, and that night, inspired by her rejection, he did just that.

The next day, after only seven hours of sleep, he returned to the princess's castle and rang the front bell. A maid answered.

"I am here to see the princess," he said. "I have a present for her. I must see her at once."

"What is your name?" asked the maid.

The plumber waited and waited, and waited and waited, but the maid did not return. He rang the doorbell again and still the maid did not answer. He started to go, but before he could reach the bus shelter a voice came calling after him.

"Come here! Come back! You give up too easily, man!"

The plumber turned but could see nobody. "Who is it?" he asked. "Who's following me?"

"It is I!" came the voice, and the plumber traced it and came face to face with a frog in a tree. "I have been watching the whole thing," said the frog, "and it's a shame the way she's been treating you. Why don't you find yourself a nice girl? There are many beautiful girls in this town."

"I don't want a nice girl," he replied. "I want the princess. Only she won't give me a chance because I'm a plumber. She doesn't see what I can do. Here, I made this," he said, and held out the wooden contraption, inspired especially by her. "If she saw it she would know what kind of man I really am."

"I know what kind of man you really are," said the frog. "You're a crazy man! What is this contraption? That won't make her love you. Women don't care about bits and gadgets. They want you to prove you're better than them. Building this ridiculous machine makes you no better than her, I say that."

The plumber looked at the frog a moment longer, then turned and walked towards the bus shelter. He was upset with what the frog had said and disinclined to believe him, but the frog had spoken so persuasively, and with such assurance. Still, what did a frog know about love? He was about to return and ask for his credentials but the bus arrived, and it only came once every twenty minutes.

On the bus there was a beautiful little girl of about seven or eight. She was carrying a rubber doll and sitting next to the only empty seat. The plumber sat next to her and her blonde pigtail rested against his bare arm. She couldn't help it; they were flyaway curls.

"Your celluloid doll," he said. "What's her name?"

The girl smiled a little smile, then turned her sad watery eyes out the window, and with a faraway look said, "I'm in the middle of a very bad nightmare. Don't speak to me, sir, please." She saw the world going by at a very high speed, and outside everything was dark and grey. Cities and towns just whooshed on by, and beside her was a giant skyscraper of a man with big burly hands. She whispered into her doll a secret that the man could not hear, but as he was afraid of saying any more, he did not ask.

He got off at his stop but her hair somehow followed him. Three little bits of it had stuck to his arm, and in bed that night they pressed against him and softly lulled him to sleep.

That night he had a sad sad dream, and when he woke in the morning he remembered about the princess. The three hairs of the girl from the bus had wound themselves into the shape of a heart above his own heart, and he lifted it with his finger and recalled what the frog had told him: "Woman wants a man who is better than herself."

He got up and went to the shower. He did not shower, though. He didn't want to start the day with such an unexceptional activity. So the plumber turned and dressed and stepped out straight into the fresh sunny air. It was springtime and still each sunny day was a present. "Hello!" he called to the birds that swooped down around him, and went straight to the castle to call on the princess.

When he arrived he could tell something was the matter. Whereas before in the air there had been riches and gaiety and pomp, on that day there was something thick and skeletal and musty. The plumber rang the bell. The maid answered, but the maid was all of a sudden quite a skinny woman.

"What happened to your body?" he couldn't help asking, aghast.

"Oh me." She looked down at the ground and her eyes welled up with tears. "I have become this way in only a day. There seems to be a plague upon the castle. All of us are shrivelling away. The butlers, the cooks, even our little princess."

"The princess!" cried the plumber. "I must see her."

"No!" cried the maid. "You must stay away from this house. It is quarantined. You will get sick if you come in, plagued with whatever plague has befallen it. Plus, she is too weak to take visitors."

"She's dying," he said softly, and immediately knew whose fault it was. He gave his condolences and pulled a few blades of grass from the lawn and threw them upon the bricks that made up the castle walls.

When he had wandered far enough away he called out, "Frog!" and patrolled the tree where he had met the frog the day before. "Come out! I know you're there! You're probably camouflaging yourself! Come out, come out!"

The frog reluctantly climbed onto a low branch from the bramble of leaves where he had been happily shading himself.

"Why are you killing the princess?" the man demanded.

"What? Who? I? I am not killing the princess. It is *you* who is killing the princess."

"What are you talking about," said the man who was a plumber and had forgotten all about his job over the last three days. If he didn't go to work soon he would surely have no job at all, and that would not be right.

"Pay attention to me now," the frog said. "The world is changing. It's a different place from when you were a boy. All of a sudden there are going to be large corporations with robots to do all the work. People will have no jobs and no use. The money the corporations make will be taxed heavily by the government, and the government will give all that money to the people. It will be a complete welfare state. At the same time, people will be living up to two hundred years, what with the advances scientists are making in ageing. The whole way we look at living will be radically altered. Nothing we know about how to live a life will apply anymore. People will have two hundred years of leisure and never have to work or do anything."

The plumber was baffled. "What are you saying?" he asked. "How do you know all this? How do you know about this and how do you know about women? I don't believe you. You have no credentials."

"You want credentials! What kind of a boor are you?" said the frog.

"You can't just spout your opinions at me. I have to save the princess."

"You'll do no saving. What can you do? You have such puerile taste. There are many beautiful and willing women in the city, and lots of them would be happy with a man like you. What are you pursuing this sickly creature for?"

"Why are you killing the princess?"

"I'm not, you are."

"I don't believe this," said the plumber, then took his leave and got on a bus and ended up sitting next to the same little girl. Her eyes looked even more frightened than before, her hair was messed up, and there were dark blue circles where there should have been soft rosy cheeks.

"I'm still in the same nightmare," she said mechanically.

"The princess doesn't love me and is dying."

He got off at his stop and the girl continued on in her nightmare. This time none of her hairs stuck to him. That night he slept a fitful sleep and when he woke in the morning the sky was a funny shade of purple.

"What's happening to this world?" he asked, and then got a dull sort of inspiration and built a box out of cardboard, but with folds such as the world had never seen.

Something was going wrong, he just did not know what or why.

That afternoon he went again to see the princess, but this time the maid answered the door and said, "You have come too late. The princess is dead. Long live the queen."

The plumber was devastated. "I'll never find love now," he said, and dragged behind him a bouquet of flowers. "I'll never love again." He sat down on a bench.

The frog, but not the same one from before, plopped down from a tree and rested its tired body on his shoulder. The frog said, "The world is changing faster and faster and I am becoming an old man. Just yesterday I had the spring of youth in my step, but today I do not even recognize my belly. I look at myself and see another frog, and I look at the frogs around me and all of them seem to be passing their lives by, doing nothing in particular, all of the time."

"It's good to think of some things, some of the time," said the man who was a plumber but had since lost that skill. He picked up from the ground a blade of grass, perhaps one he had thrown on the castle for luck the day before.

The grass said nothing, just lay in his hand. He examined it but received no wisdom.

"The world is changing," he said, "but love stays the same."

That made some things better, for some of the time. The man dropped his head to his chest and wept and wept like a child, and the sky let the snow fall. And the man stopped crying like the snow stopped snowing, and the whole world was covered in white.

MERMAID IN THE JAR

I have a mermaid in a jar that Quilty bought me at a garage sale for twenty-five cents. The mermaid's all, "I hate you I hate you I hate you," but she's in a jar, and unless I loosen the top she's not coming out to kill me.

I keep the little jar on my windowsill, right behind my bed, right near my head so if I look up in the middle of the night, up and back, I can see her swimming in the murky little pool of her own shit and vomit, and I can smile.

"Hello, mermaid! How are you this fine evening?" I can say, and sometimes do. "How very sad it is that you're so beautiful, and you're so young, and you're so fucking trapped you'll never get out of that bottle, ha ha!"

Once I went on a class trip and brought my mermaid along, just for the hell of it. We were going to Niagara Falls and I was thinking, "Right, well, maybe I'll hold her over the rail, give her a little scare, put her in her place." Or letting her loose down the falls and out of my life. But once we got there I forgot her in my little brown lunchbag with my hot

11

cheese sandwich, under my seat in the yellow school bus. But she got jolted on the ride there and jolted on the ride back and that was enough for me.

Once I had a party and invited all my friends, seven little girls to play and sleep over, and having called every number flashing in our heads, and having already called the pizzas twice and seanced out of our minds, I just thought, "Oh, why don't I bring my mermaid out to show? They could make their faces at it, they could have their fun, and we'd be able to toss it back and forth like a real little football." But then Emma fell asleep, and then so did Wendy and Carla and the rest, and the mermaid just stayed locked in the closet where I'd put her that afternoon.

Once when I thought she needed a bit of discipline I rolled her measly bottle down Killer Hill in the ravine. Another time I threw her deep into my best friend's pool.

Now she's getting old it seems. I even saw a grey hair on Friday, and wrinkles are spreading all across her skin, and as much as I liked her before, I like her even less now. I was thinking sort of what to do with her, but I think I'll just keep her there a little while longer. At least until I'm happy again.

THE MISS AND SYLVIA AND SAM

A frivolous young Miss, who was a little bit proper and a little bit delicate, stopped at a flea market stand and picked up a bottle and said to the woman, "And how much is this?"

"Seventy-five cents."

"And how much is this?"

"Four dollars."

"And how much is this thing?"

"A dollar ninety-five."

"I'll take it."

She went on in that manner for the whole entire day, just wandering through stalls, lifting up buttons and handbags and monocles, and thinking nothing greater than, "And how much is this thing?" "And how much is this thing?" "And how much is this?"

When she got home that night she arranged everything she had bought on her little kitchen table, and tallied in her head the amount she had spent — seventy-four dollars and twenty-five cents — and took up the items separately in her hands and began to clean them one by one. First there was the feather baton, then the little top hat, then the picture frame with the picture in it.

After a few hours she yawned adorably and lifted up her arms. When she woke in the morning she returned to the market. One of the women at one of the stalls, an oval thing with a bob of grey hair, said to the Miss, "Hello. I think I know you. You look very familiar to me."

"Yes," replied the Miss. "I probably am. I was here yesterday."

"No," said the woman from behind the stall, and she put her hands on the glass and leaned a bit forward. "I feel I know you from another life."

"Oh, that's impossible!" laughed the Miss. "This is the only life I've had." She had heard about women like this before, women who believed in reincarnation, though she'd never actually spoken to one. She felt unsure of how to act. "Good-bye," she said, by way of explanation, and moved precisely down the aisle.

The woman ran out from behind the table and grabbed the Miss by the arm. "Wait!"

"Ow!"

"I know you from another life!"

"I told you! I was here yesterday," said the Miss, and she pulled her arm from the woman's grip.

"But I've had dreams about you."

"No, that's ridiculous. I don't believe in any of that

14

stuff." And the Miss turned and lost herself in the bustle, not looking back. The woman slowly returned to her stall, but kept her eyes on the delicate form that was not being kind.

That night, as the Miss was falling asleep, a ring came from the telephone. She felt too tired to pick it up, but on the seventh ring she did. After all, it could have been her new boyfriend, who was so new he was practically not even a real boyfriend at all.

"Yes?" she said into the receiver.

"This is Sam."

"Hello!" she squealed, brightening and sitting up a little. "I was just falling asleep."

"Were you thinking of me?"

"Of course I was." She began to blush and played with the neck of her nightie a bit. "I was thinking it would be you. I'm psychic you know."

"You're not psychic. What are you wearing?"

She told him the nightie's colour and texture. Then she said, "And how was your day?"

"Can I come over?" His voice was a bit of a whine.

"No!" she said, quite astonished. "It's nearly one in the morning!"

"But you're up, aren't you?"

"No," she said. "It wouldn't be appropriate." They said a few more words to each other and then she fell asleep, a little bit perturbed.

In the morning, as the sun was tiptoeing in through the blinds and she was shifting in her sheets, a knock came from the door. "Oh, darn," she said, and pulled on her new bathrobe and pulled on her slippers, which also were brand-new and red, and went down the hall to answer it. "Who is it?" she asked as she was unfastening the chain, but when she saw who it was she cried, "Oh, no!" and pushed her weight against the door. "This is not right," she said through the wood, and was about to fasten the lock when the visitor popped herself in and slammed the door shut.

"I haven't been following you," said the woman from the market, who seemed to have dyed her hair overnight, for now it was orange, not grey. "We have a friend in common: Sam."

"Sam!"

"Sam's my brother," said the woman lightly. "Can I sit down?"

"Why—" The Miss was nervous. "Sam's not your brother!"

Three weeks later the whole thing was arranged. The Miss was going to marry Sam, and Sylvia, the woman from the market (who remarkably had the same middle name as the Miss), was going to be the flower girl.

Sitting around a card table under a dim light, Sylvia went on throwing out her thoughts. "I've always wanted to be a flower girl! All my life! Remember when we thought Uncle Murray was going to get married, and I was going to be a flower girl and then he never did, and the whole wish just floated away?"

"You're real funny," said Sam, smiling. He hadn't stopped smiling since he had met the Miss, and now the two were leaning into each other, and grinning so broadly, and giving each other sweet little looks out of the corners of their eyes. Sylvia rested back in her chair across from them, and she was all smiles too. "I'm so happy for you both. I'm so happy. I just know it's going to work out."

"I'm going to help Sylvia with the business," said the Miss eagerly, as though Sam had never heard it.

"I know, I know."

"She's really going to do it, Sam!"

"I know!"

The Miss had always loved antiques, and now she was going to help with the business! It really was something else.

That Saturday, Sylvia and the Miss were down at the market, standing under a cloudy sky, resting their heels behind the table, when a woman came up to them. She was similar in colour and build to the Miss, and she kept her eyes on the table, touching ornaments from Christmases half a century before. "How much is this?" "And how much is this?" "And how much is this?" It was a horrible day and suddenly it began to rain. Everyone started packing up their wares to move them quickly inside. "But how much is this! And how much is this!" Her terrible eyes were brown and fierce and she pushed her face towards them as they hurried to box it all up.

"You can follow us inside," said Sylvia harshly. "We have to get these items in before they're soaked by the rain."

But the woman didn't want to leave. "I want to buy these ornaments!" she cried.

The Miss was getting scared.

Sylvia repeated, "You must wait till we're inside! Please stay out of our way."

"This is inexcusable! I'm a valid shopper!"

"Oh, please don't fight!" cried the Miss, her eyes all alight, her whole chest fluttering. "Don't fight. Don't fight. You can have them for twenty dollars, the set." She glanced at Sylvia for approval, but Sylvia only rolled her eyes. She was trying to get everything into boxes.

"Good," said the woman. "Thank you. That's the courtesy I was looking for." And she reached into her bag to get the money, but before she could pull out the bills a tiny thunderbolt came from the sky and shot straight down through the woman shopper's head, striking her to the ground.

"Good God!" screamed the Miss, and she fell to her knees, shrieking and sobbing hysterically, patting her fingers against the charred-up body. "She was just standing here! Just standing here!" She continued to bawl as the rain poured down. harder and harder, drenching everyone and everything.

Sylvia continued to put away objects, but she was nervous and spooked. She said quietly to herself, "I don't understand. I told her to go. I told her not to hang about."

The wedding was three weeks away. As they gathered around a fountain, talking over plans, it was Sylvia who came up with all the ideas and who was the most excited. The Miss and Sam mostly sat there holding each other. "What a marvellous day," the Miss kept saying. "What a beautiful marvellous day with tons of sun!"

When the wedding came, Sylvia gave a little speech that was squeaky and uncertain, and the Miss got drunk on dry white wine and ended up sleeping near the cake.

Cleaning their room the next morning, Sylvia suddenly stood upright and said to them, "I'm going now. I'm moving to Hamilton for three whole years. I don't know when I'll see you again."

"Hamilton!" cried the Miss, who had grown to like Sylvia. "But why?"

"Better fairs," explained Sylvia. Then she dropped her hands in her pockets. "Everything is cleared up. The cake is in the fridge. I must go now. I want to get the prime spot." And she kissed them both on the cheek and disappeared.

The Miss and Sam lay in bed, licking each other's bodies. Then he turned her over and took her from behind.

The next day, as they were leaving for Israel to go on their honeymoon, Sam said, "There's just one thing I forgot to tell you, dear."

"What?" exclaimed the Miss, not afraid but anxious. "What is it?"

He smiled. "That's the whole point, darling. I forgot."

She shook her head and widened her eyes. What a strange and awful man, she thought. Then she checked her bag. The tickets were still there.

THE WOMAN WHO LIVED IN A SHOE

She was only a woman living in a shoe, and she didn't understand the ways of the world. Didn't know how to act at every specific social gathering. Wasn't invited to many anymore, not even museum openings.

One day a man came to her shoe and knocked on the front door. She went to open it and saw an older fellow who was quite charming-looking. He was holding a huge burst of roses and smiling at her, and she smiled back from inside.

"Why . . ." she said.

"I love you Dora," said the man, and he held out the flowers, and they were so grand and vast that they blocked her face entirely.

She was a modest woman and did not know what to say.

"Say you'll marry me."

"I can't," said the woman. She had said this before. "There's only room for me in the shoe, and if I leave, it will disappear and fall to the ground out of sorrow and uselessness."

The man turned and went away.

21

"Wait!" she called after him, waving her hand, but he kept walking in such a sorrow because he really did love Dora, and it was not good enough if she just kind of liked him back. He was the one she had to worry about falling to the ground out of sorrow and uselessness, not the shoe.

Well, there were a number of opportunities for the woman to have fun, and go to public events and make herself known to the world as the woman she was. But whenever she was invited she would just look at the card and shake her head. "I'd have nothing to wear," she'd say to herself, placing her hand against the leather walls. "And who would I meet there? And if I did, then what?"

Then the woman who lived in a shoe would go outside and sit on the toe and watch as the world went by in all its busy activity: the cities making money and the sun as it so very quickly went up in the sky and down in the sky and up and down and up and down like a yo-yo.

"My," she would say to herself. "I don't know how anybody finds any time to do anything in a day." And she'd go back inside her shoe where it was one colour of light and smelled of leather, and she'd knit or stitch or wring her hands, or not, or play cards with herself, or not.

One day the woman put up a notice on the door of the shoe. When the mailman came by he shook his head and walked away, saying to himself, "It's a changing world. Without the shoe it'll be any normal street, any normal city, any normal day. There will be a great tall tower put up there, and it will be the burial ground of the shoe. And I'll never see another woman who lives in a shoe ever again, and every shoe I see forever more will be just a shoe, just a shoe."

Then the baker came by with a loaf of bread that he had been making every week for twenty years, perfectly sized for the woman who lived in a shoe. "No shoe!" he exclaimed, and hugged the bread in close to his chest. As the tears welled up in his eyes he started to pull off nibbles. And when the milkman came by to drop off a milk bottle, something he did only for the woman who lived in a shoe, he took several stunned steps back, shaking his head like all the rest. His heart was filled with an inexpressible sorrow, and he looked at the shoe, and at the horizon, and back at the shoe, and back at the horizon.

That was all very well. When the woman came out she found no bread, she found no mail, she found no milk, and she found no men. So she took down the sign, picked up her suitcase, and looked into the distance at the city with the watch setting over the hill. She left the door open as she walked from the shoe, and walked and walked and walked and walked and walked and walked and walked and walked. There was little one could do in a day, in the outside world, outside the shoe.

THE MIDDLEMAN TO ELDA

The middleman was very confident these days, having just been given a big salary, and having just found a blonde-haired woman he liked and could talk to. The other night in bed the blonde-haired woman had said to him, "Come now, no more of that," and had pushed away his head. But this did not bother the middleman as he strode down the street with the sun on his face and his shoes all asparkle.

"It's a good day for me," he said to himself. "Yup, a good day for me." And not even the blonde woman's pushy hand could take that feeling away from him.

He passed a bird. He passed a very interesting ramshackle house and a house that was beautiful, and he thought, "I'd like to live there." Then he continued walking with a more purposeful expression, when suddenly he felt a pain in his heart from the night before.

"She pushed away my face," he realized, stopping short as the feeling of horror and humiliation welled up in him.

"It's not good, it's not good." He hadn't realized it at all until now. Rushing back in the other direction he hopped on a bus to her part of town, a ratty neighbourhood with garbage cans and soot. He climbed the fire escape to her room, which was crisscrossed in the window with brightly coloured stockings.

"Elda!" he cried through the window from the tiny landing on which he was standing. "Elda! Elda!" He had to speak to her quick.

Elda sauntered over. "Why Henry," she said.

The middleman took a step back. "May I come inside? I must speak with you."

"Why sure," said Elda, and she stepped away. The middleman took one quick look at her before he entered: she looked high.

"Have you been smoking, Elda?" he asked, as he pulled in his wiry legs behind him. "You've been smoking drugs, haven't you?" he asked, sniffing the air.

"And what if I have?" She put up her nose defiantly.

"Nothing, nothing, Elda," he said, and he pulled her down on the couch beside him, holding her hands in his own. "I regret everything!" And he explained it all at once. "I have tried to be the man for you but in trying I have not been a man at all, and I have been nothing and not myself, and I regret it — I regret it all terribly. Can we start again? Can you ever forget the man I was until right now — my deceit?"

"Deceit?" she asked lazily.

"I understand fully why you did what you did. It was

what you had to do. I was inconsiderate. You have been good and honest with me and I have been playing a game. Look at me! I'm a fool! But I'm coming here knowing my humiliation is certain and risking that you may not love me for this, but I love you too much not to say it, Elda. I had to say it."

"What are you saying?"

He looked at her deeply, puzzled, perplexed. "But Elda. Haven't you seen how I've been behaving with you? Like a real country gentleman! But *this* is the real me! This is the real me! Not the man from before! Me, here, as I'm representing myself to you now!"

"Fine," she said, shrugging her shoulders. Then, seeing his distress was real, she leaned in close and looked into his eyes, pressing her hands down on his knees. "Really. It's fine."

He looked at her blankly.

"Fine," he said, and stood up.

"Really, it's fine," she said lazily, standing up behind him and moving in front of him to open the door.

"Well I'm glad," he said, walking out. "I have letters to write," he said, and walked out.

THE FUNDAMENTAL RACE

"There is exactly one of everything in the world. A tulip that looks around and finds its position to be lacking some cannot go and become a rose. Do not be afraid to be a rose, Lila. If indeed you are one."

This was part of what he had been saying all morning and trying to impress upon poor Lila: that there are no copycats in nature.

Lila was a terrible student. She looked at the teacher with a face of dubious confusion. Though she knew nothing and learned nothing, she was willing and handed in her essays on time. Her teacher was one of seventeen she had ever had. His name was Mr. Phelps. He lived alone and his wife came to visit him with pies of every nature three times a week. His current project was How to Get It Through Her Head.

"By looking at a rose you do not turn a little more red," he gave as one example. "Loving the song of the bird doesn't give you a more beautiful voice. You are locked in. All humans are locked in. Each human is a species unto itself.

Comparing yourself with anyone — even if she is your age and has curlier, blonder hair — is like pitting pigs against toads. You would not pit a pig against a toad, right?"

She showed that she agreed with him on this fine point but did not change her expression, so he was not convinced.

He asked her patiently, "In what situation would you pit a pig against a toad?"

She hated learning.

Her mother was a terrible woman and permitted Lila to sit with her feet on the table. She let the girl beat her in sports because she just didn't care. Lila never got any better this way, and one of her mother's suitors thought, upon meeting Lila, that she had been born retarded. But she was not retarded; she just hadn't been given the proper care. Of course, she did not accept the proper care. Like all things, she determined the rules of her own existence. Her mother couldn't prevent Lila from being the way she was. But that didn't stop those who knew the situation from criticizing her anyway, fundamentally, for letting such a life exist.

Lila ordered a bouquet of roses and sat with them at her vanity table and looked at them as though, as her teacher had suggested, they were an alien species. She wouldn't compare them to a bucket of water. She wouldn't compare them to a snail. She liked snails; they had shells they could curl themselves into. Roses had no shells. But roses were romantic.

On her speed-dial princess phone she called up a boy she

had met once, several years ago. He had heard from her monthly, sometimes weekly, since they had danced together that one time. Already he was somewhere on his way to becoming a lawyer, if he wasn't a lawyer already. His girlfriend was very sleek and not at all lumpy; a girlfriend to be proud of. She had slick brown hair, not at all the sort of hair that one found on imported dolls.

He was exasperated when he found out it was Lila.

"You sent me roses," she said.

"Can't you tell I can't stand you!!" he cried, in a voice he used with nobody except her. She deserved it. She looked into the receiver and one contained bit of her sobbed uncontrollably at the tone he used, but the rest of her was blank with dumb confusion. She didn't know what to make of it. Who was he again? She put the receiver to her ear and heard a click and then a silence. Her tongue lolled slightly behind her lip as she hung up the phone. She would not pit a cow against a bouquet of roses. Whatever for? The cow would win, surely.

THE LITTLEST DUMPLING

A sad little dumpling who had never been told his name started off his day by dropping softly to the ground and lying there.

Because he was bruised he started to cry and held himself as best he could, rocking a little back and forth.

"Oh, my sore little self," he moaned, and looked up at the pot in which his brothers and sisters were floating, and felt sad and alone.

"I'll never see them again," he feared, and rolled under the centre of the table and lay there with thumb in his mouth, crying himself to sleep ever so gently.

It was only six in the morning and already the whole world was becoming pastel with the sun rising from behind the clouds, painting everything pink or blue or light light yellow.

When the newspaper arrived, thumping down on the stoop outside the house, the toilet flushed from upstairs and the father came down and opened the door, letting a gust of cool air in. He picked up the bundle, snapped the elastic off, and sat down on the couch to read.

There were terrible stories all throughout the paper, stories about people killing each other and hurting each other, people playing the wrong kinds of music and saying the wrong things. Even something about deaths. Even some jokes and predictions. But there was nothing about the dumpling. The man had no idea that the littlest dumpling from his very own pot had fallen onto his kitchen floor and was there, right now, tears in his eyes.

When the son came down he went into the kitchen to get his orange juice and milk and cereal. He called out to his father to see if he wanted any, but the father said no, just a banana, and there was no mention of the dumpling. Probably they weren't planning on eating the dumplings until later that night.

The father sat at the table and the son sat across from him, and the first ray of light fell straight through the window into the dumpling's eyes, waking him up at once. He tried not to move, tried not to seem dangerous, and tried not to scare them back.

The father said some booming things to the son, and the son said some booming things also, and the sounds and the words reverberated inside the littlest dumpling, and the dumpling felt littler, then littler, then suddenly big enough.

But by then the father and son had gone from the table,

and the dumpling looked down at himself with disgust.

"Now, what was I afraid of! Damn it! What was I so damn afraid of!"

He uncurled and stretched himself out to full length, cursing. "I should have just crawled on his shoe, up his leg, just stood on his knee and made myself clear!"

After a couple of moments the front door slammed and there was a silence. Now the dumpling was all alone. Lying there he felt exhausted. It had already been quite an ordeal and he'd still have to get back in the pot. Such a feat would be practically impossible, though, because in the several hours since he had fallen out he had lost his stick and would not be able to make it even halfway up the stove. The littlest dumpling was drying out.

When he realized this — *drying out!* — he froze, shuddered, then seized some more. Drying out was the worst sort of death, a long and painful one! There would be no escape; the father and son would not be home for several hours. He would die, then be swept up perhaps a week later.

Unfair. That's what they always said about life. Who said it was fair? Who said you could do what you wanted? There were ways of doing things, ways to die. The dumpling was just a dumpling and the family was just a family.

THE FAVOURITE MONKEY

They lay under the tree in the morning June air and breathed in each other's whispers. That's how romantic it was under the tree — under any tree! And nobody made them leave or shake it off.

Already they had found out the meaning of life and the meaning of their love, and they had only met three days before, as he was sunning himself under the tree and she fell from its branches.

"Hello!" she had said, and he had said, "Hello," and that's when they knew they would always understand each other, even though she was a monkey.

He called her "my little monkey" when he brought her home from the hill, and they lay in his bed and made up secrets to tell each other, so they would have something sweet and pure to reveal.

She told him lies that made him happy and made her happier, and he told her fairy stories that made her sigh in admiration of him, for he had made up such beautiful stories just for her.

He wasn't very smart, but could feel people's hearts by being near them, and he said, "Dear monkey, I do so hate living in the city. I can hear the trees crying." And when the monkey heard this she began to cry, for him and the trees, but for him, mostly, that he should feel such pain.

She was very sad three days later when she told him that her mother was calling and she had to get back, just to say she was fine and had fallen in love with a beautiful boy and was going to live with him forever. But the boy cried and held the monkey's hand and said, "Don't go! Don't go! You'll never come back! I love you and I need you!" And his eyes threw tears onto the floor and the walls, and he sobbed into his bedspread while the monkey patted his back and said soothingly into his ear, "I love you, I love you. I'll be back in a day and a night, after I tell my mother, and then we'll live happily ever after." And the monkey grinned and a twinkle came into her eye, but the boy was still sad, and he kissed the monkey feverishly and held onto her fur and finally let go, watching from the window as she climbed up and over the hill.

With the monkey gone the boy just lay in his bed, and though his friends came calling, he did not answer. He was content to be alone and think of the monkey.

But his friends did not understand; they were persistent and continued to knock on the door, crying, "Let us in! Let us in!" And though the boy did not want to, at last he relented because they just wouldn't stop, and besides, he wanted to share his happiness.

The boys had been his friends for a long long time, and they saw, at once, that he really had found love, and they sat on wooden chairs and made happy silent faces when he told them about the monkey who would soon be his wife, and though they were boys, they made no crass remarks.

When the boy had said all there was to say and there was nothing left to reveal, one of his friends said, "Let's go for a drink."

"Oh no," replied the boy. "I must stay here and wait for my monkey. Who knows when she'll be back. You go. I'm happy to lie on my bed and think of her."

"No, no," said his friend, and the others chimed in, "Come on, come on, come out with us." They missed the boy and worried they might never see him again.

But he said no and refused.

Yet still the friends kept prodding and begging, "Come on, come on, you're not saying no," and so finally, reluctantly, the boy gave in, and he put on his shirt and shoes and left, locking the door behind him.

The boys took him to a little tavern with a red-peaked roof, and they sat outside in the cool spring air. The night was dark, and they couldn't see the hill, but they could see the stars. And the boy said wonderful things, and they all said sorrowful things, smart things and funny things, and they laughed and laughed and got quite drunk, and at three in the morning the boys stumbled home, down the cobblestones into the town, but the boy returned to his little cabin and opened the door and walked inside and fell into bed.

When he woke in the morning he felt sick and drunk, but when he remembered that his monkey would be arriving home, he got up and washed and put on a shirt and sat at the table and ate a banana and waited.

Then he went to his porch and waited there, so that he could see his monkey as she approached. But soon the day grew dark and the boy grew concerned. "It's impossible," he thought. "She loves me as much as I love her. The looks in her eyes — she couldn't have been pretending. No, no." Those were the kinds of thoughts he was saying to himself as he waited, now on his bed, now in the darkness, now inside and under the sheets. "Her mother is probably a nag and wants to keep her there. Maybe she has to sneak out at night. Maybe she has to wait for nightfall. She'll be back in the morning — I know it." And he closed his eyes and fell asleep.

In the morning the boy woke and knew he was disturbed about something. "Now what was it?" he asked, then with a panic cried, "My monkey!" He leaped from the bed and flung open the door but no one was there. "Where is she?" he bawled, and slumped down to the floor and lay in such a sorrow, crying, "My beautiful monkey, my beautiful monkey, the only girl I ever loved," singing soothing songs to himself, making up the tunes as he went along.

At about one in the afternoon the monkey arrived.

"Hello!" she called out, and the boy pulled himself from the floor and saw his beautiful little monkey standing before him, holding a bright red suitcase.

40

"You came back!" he cried, and took her in his arms and threw her up into the air and swung her around as the monkey laughed and laughed.

"Yes, I'm back. I'm sorry I was late," she said, and put down her suitcase and went and sat on the bed.

The boy followed and took her hand in his. "Oh, I was so scared. I thought you'd never show up. I missed you so much and I love you so much. Please, please, never leave me again. I'd die without you. I'd really really die."

And he went on and on like that as she sat with her hand in his, smiling at his face, waiting for him to finish.

THE GIANT

There was a giant in their town. His name was Sal. Everybody laughed as he walked by and said things like, "Hey giant!" and waved and grinned and elbowed their dates in the ribs and stuff like that, which the giant tolerated only because he was a giant. It was part of his lot to be way way bigger than everybody and teased mercilessly for being so.

His parents, Jewish, normal-sized, let him stay at home with them. There was no way he was going to find a wife, no way a woman would want to jeopardize her life for him, and so they coddled him and treated him like a little boy.

One day the giant said to his mother, "I'm thinking of killing myself."

It was a dark day in their household then. The mother told the father and the two of them sat with their son in the living room and gave him a big long talk.

The father said, "Maybe you just need to see the world. This small town can get a little oppressive at times. Why don't you take your bag and hat and go. Your mother and I

43

have money. Don't worry about us."

And the giant looked at his mother and saw her nodding at him, and the giant wept and wept at the kindness of his parents.

Three days later he was ready and the day after that he left, his mother and father waving him good-bye at the train station.

Since he was a giant, accommodations were a little difficult. In the train he had to sit with the feed, and on the boat he had to stay on the deck, but when he got to Paris he was free, walking around in the bright sunny air with all the other people, tourists and natives alike. He couldn't stop smiling. He had no idea that such a world lay beyond his small town, especially a world where people spoke differently and looked at him without cruelty. He met up with a bunch of rowdy young men on his first night there and they all went to a bar where they got quite drunk. It was the first time the giant had ever been drunk and he was quite pleased with the sensation. He told them that he loved them, that they were the first friends he had ever had, and the one who spoke English translated for the rest, and they all let out a cheer and clanked their mugs together, and the giant felt right at home.

The next day the giant wandered through the streets and was surprised to find a demure young woman in a light-blue dress bending over a balcony, watching him as he passed. She called to him, "Please come!"

The giant, who knew a little French, crossed the street and laid his head on the railing and looked brightly into her eyes. She touched his nose and laughed out loud, then pet his eyes and pet his hair, then covered his face with kisses and ran inside squealing.

Well, the giant had never been kissed by a woman before, and whether or not he'd see her again was a worry for another time. He just strolled into a park and lay down on the grass and relived the sensation over and over.

Suddenly he realized it was two o'clock.

"Oh, no!" he cried. "If I don't catch the boat I'll be ruined!"

He ran down to the dock and caught it just as it was about to leave the harbour, then settled on the deck and watched Paris recede.

The next day he was home again.

His mother and father sat him down in the living room.

"And how was your trip?" his father asked.

The giant smiled. "I said I was never coming home, and I'm not," he thought.

THE GIRL WHO
WAS BLIND ALL THE TIME

She lived in the hollow of her mouth and ears. She lived in the two deep hollows of her nose, and when and if someone touched her, she lived in her skin as well.

She made her way to and from school each day. She had no dog. She didn't want to be led by a beast, she said, and people laughed. That's all they really did around her. Laugh. Because you can't just smile, and you have to be nice to a blind girl.

She got dizzy when she thought of sex, which she had never had, and she got dizzy when she thought of boys, and so she didn't think of them very often.

She once held her own one-woman parade down the long winding road that circled her university campus, and she carried a flag with the word "See," and she marched on by, and had no idea for weeks afterwards what the response was, if any. Only when Julie phoned and read to her some little news item in the *University Bulletin* that said, "Blind

47

Girl Leads Revolution Single-Handedly," did she grimace and go, "Oh God," and go, "Nobody has any fucking sense of humour." And Julie, over the phone, laughed.

The blind girl went to parties but always with a girlfriend, and always her girlfriend would return to her, and the blind girl would say, "Go away, have your fun." Sometimes her friend caught her talking to a guy, sometimes her friend caught her standing all alone.

The blind girl never once thought about suicide and was surprised when a boy brought it up. "Don't you ever think of killing yourself?" he asked, and then she put it to all her friends for the next few weeks. "Well do *you* ever think of killing yourself?" And they all answered yes.

She was surprised.

She started to think about it herself.

She said to herself, "Suicide," and mulled the word over, and thought, "But how would I ever do it?" And after three weeks of thinking about it, she knew how. She'd walk off a bridge. She'd kill herself just like that.

After that month of suicide thoughts she had three of the best days of her life. She met a boy, fell in love, lay out in the sunshine and held his hand and kissed, and fucked behind a video store, and after those three days she had the worst year ever, the worst year of her whole entire life. A year she would look back on when she was eighty and still think, "Yep, that was the worst fucking year of my whole entire life."

Every day she was sick and green and every day she woke

up with a foul smell in her nose, which ebbed in and out from morning till night, and her glands swelled up and she cried and cried, and her friends started calling more and more often, then stopped. And her belly swelled up and her hair sweated down her back, and her mother yelled about money and her future, and she ran into walls, and she fell down stairs, and was disoriented, and lost, like a girl gone blind.

She came out of that year very skinny and very tattered. Almost all of her bones had been broken or banged and she had welts and bruises everywhere, especially on her face, and dark black circles under her eyes. And the thought of parading around campus with a joke flag made her quiver with nausea and resentment.

That was it. She came out of it. She never had such a down as that or such an up as the three days that preceded it, not ever again in her life. The rest of her life was like a long thin line with little diminuendos and tiny little crescendos and friends visiting from out of town.

She had a big, bright, curly head of hair that made her look like a clown, and nobody ever told her.

THE MOON MONOLOGUE

Nobody ever accused me of being bright, which I am glad for. You see, all the really bright people I have ever known have been involved in elaborate drug deals, and I'm not one of those people who believes that drugs are just a part of life. I am very much against drugs, and I think the people who do them are foolish. I have seen the way they make people act, and I am not a space case. I am a genuine human being, and I express what I'm feeling.

So when it happened that Bobby, that night in the cellar, touched my breast with the palm of his hand and fell back as though electric-shocked and said, "You're bright, Marie!" I thought he was the biggest goof ever, and I said so.

"Nobody's ever accused *me* of being bright, Bobby," I said with pride and a bit of anger. I got up and went straight to my room to watch the sun rise, but there was another hour still to go. I just sat at the window then, and looked out at the lawn and thought it was a pretty confusing world, which it is, if you look at it the right way.

So much for that.

It wasn't two days later before I began meeting people on the street who started asking me questions; questions about where the world was going to, what would be happening with plants in the future, and would pets be obsolete soon? Strangely enough, I had all the right answers for these people. It was like they had put the ideas in my mind with the questions they were asking. "Sure," I said. "There's all sorts of things that'll happen in the future."

"Like what, Marie?"

"Well, I'll tell you. Tomorrow I'm going to a party and I'm going to be the hit of that party. I'm going to wear a dress and make out crazily with all the boys. The boys I know are pretty sly but they can't pass anything over on me. If I see Bobby I'm just going to ignore his face."

Anyway, it turned out some kind of expedition was coming up and they wanted three pretty girls from our town. It was to colonize a new community, somewhere in the middle of the ocean where no people had ever been. I'm not one of the prettiest girls, not even in my school, but I decided I was going to go. If everyone else was going to go.

Just so turns out I did go, and guess who was chosen? Me and two others! Two girls I didn't know but who said to me privately, like in confession, that they thought *I* was the prettiest of the bunch. Well, imagine that! Me with my misshaped tooth and my hair of straw. If that wasn't the craziest thing I'd ever heard!

Just so happened that we went and ended up staying

three whole years. When we got back Bobby was married to that slut from the prom. Turns out they even had a kid on the way. When Bobby saw me he pulled me by the hand into a little parkette and said, "Look at you. You're miraculous."

I had gotten a bit of confidence in that time, and I said, all cheeky and indifferent, "I know."

Now it so happens that Bobby is making me his lover on the side. I'm having a real good time fucking him and all. I learned all sorts of crazy things in the colonies, and one of them is about fucking, about how asses really matter.

One day I'm going to the moon, and when I go, I'm going to bring back a teaspoon of sugar.

The Party at Her Place, with Her Piano

The girl played the piano as everyone found their corner, or their spot in the alley out by the house, and the neighbourhood women leaned through their windows to yell, lights on, curlers in their hair. The girl had a famous piano-playing brother whom she never stopped thinking about, even in moments of relaxation, and never let her friends stop thinking about, even when buying drugs.

When she went to the front door after her set, climbing over bodies, spilled beer, all that, she met two boys. One she had known from an old friend's breakup, the other she had never seen before. He was tall and lanky with mystery in his eyes, a cigarette in his hand, and the perfect entrance, and she fell instantly in love and forgot about her brother.

"Hello," she squeaked, then scurried away.

The boy walked in tall and smooth, did not climb over anybody's legs, and made his way to a wall upstairs to pose against while the other one found a circle of friends to show off his drunkenness to.

The girl was lost for several minutes. No one knew where she had gone. When the music returned she was found back at the piano with no audience waiting, and the boy she had been preparing for was nowhere to be seen.

She ran downstairs and out the door. There he stood in the alley, smoking a joint with several guys and two pretty girls, who laughed and huddled; their own little party.

The boy looked over and she forgot her successful brother, who was not only successful but gay, and successful at that too, and probably fucking right now, and she looked down at her boot and stammered, "Oh, nothing, nothing," and jolted her body and shook her head and walked inside.

The drunken boy who had been entertaining was now tired of that and went up to the girl and said, "Hey, come on, play the piano for us. Come on, come on," dragging her by the hand.

"Who's your friend? Is he the one you're living with now? Is he the one you're living with?" she asked, sitting down at the piano. "He seems awfully shy or strange or something."

"Play!" he demanded, then plunked himself down and put his hands on the keys and began a song, the tedious song that everyone knows.

"No, come on," she pushed him off. "Get away." And she played her own song, and it was not her brother's; it was low and romantic and moody, and she sang aloud in a halting way. Her voice was into it, trembling and all that, but her soul was looking out for the boy, her heart was searching the room.

Her lyrics were terrible and finally she stopped. No one was listening anyway. She went downstairs and back outside but the boy was gone and so was the group, and she ran inside but found neither of the boys.

"Have they gone?" she asked a girl who ought to have known. "Where'd they go? Did they leave?"

"I think they left. He thought the party sucked."

"Oh." She walked outside and looked down the alley, then went back in. "They really left."

"That's what I told you. Is your brother in town?"

The girl answered as she had before, looking around. She talked about his plans in LA, who he was meeting, what he would be wearing for his good-bye concert.

And the boys down the block, turning onto the next block, said nothing to each other.

One had nothing in his mind, the other just had nothing.

THE GIRL WHO PLANTED FLOWERS

When she woke in the morning there beside her was the boy she had dismissed the night before as far too ugly and ingratiating, and on the other side, even more of a surprise, the boy she had dismissed as far too pompously intellectual. And there she was in the middle, and she thought she was in the house where she had partied the night before, but she wasn't sure, she just wasn't sure.

She climbed gingerly over the one and went to the window and looked out into the backyard where she saw huge piles of sand, little mountains with peaks. And as she had no idea why or where they had come from, she quickly decided, "I must have blacked out." Then she went to the bathroom and returned as the two boys were rising.

"Hello boys," she said lazily, without surprise or enthusiasm. And the boys, first one, then the other, said hello and looked at each other, but as they did not smile or seem to commiserate, the girl took her seat at the foot of the bed.

"I'm hungry," she said. "Are you two hungry?"

One boy nodded while clearing the sleep out of his eyes, and the other boy looked around trying to figure out where he was.

"Well then, let's go," she said. And since they were all in their clothes there was nothing to do but leave.

One boy was taller, and the three moved slowly down the road. It was cold. It was already November and should have been colder, but still, it was cold, and the girl thought nothing. When the sidewalk narrowed the intellectual hung back, and the ugly boy and the girl walked ahead.

After five minutes they reached a good place to eat. It had eggs, it seemed, and bacon and potatoes and unlimited coffee and no sign that forbade smoking, so they took a booth at the back, and the booth was brown, and the lighting was dim, and the sun wasn't shining, and they were all wretched and existing in various degrees of humility and banality.

They all ordered the same thing, except for the ugly boy who was a vegan, and he ordered nothing but black coffee and orange juice, and the girl thought drearily in her head, "Oh God, I slept with a vegan." And the tall intelligent boy kept his eyes on the table and said nothing, and none of them said anything except the girl, who made comments like, "Are you sure you don't know what happened last night?" and "Your name is Martin, I think I remember."

Eventually she grew irritated with their silent and purposeful ignorance, their childish posturing, and she thought that since they weren't fessing up to anything, probably something like this had never happened to them before, but the thought was so terrible she pushed it from her mind.

"Well," she said when the food arrived, and inwardly cursed these humourless boys, and their dark moods succeeded in pulling her down with them, and she knew, even then, that it would be much better if they were cocky and glowing and gay.

They ate their food in silence, and the intellectual, she could tell, wanted terribly to go. Before he was finished he asked for the bill, and the young waiter brought it and left, and the intellectual left while she was still eating. Then the ugly boy gulped down the rest of his juice and paid and left, and neither said more than "okay" or "good-bye."

She was alone. She put down her money and realized for the second time that she was out of cigarettes, and felt horrible and hung over and nothing like a slut.

The girl walked through the city that day, and it was cold and dark, and the sky was uglier than it had ever been, but not as ugly as the boy she had slept with, and she realized that she was twenty-one, and she thought of her life, "What a waste." And nothing convinced her otherwise.

ELEANOR

Eleanor was fine, but she had troubles fitting in with the family at first. The young boys looked at her as though she had never had sex, which wasn't true. When she was nineteen she had slept with her boyfriend many times.

In those improbable days he was always hanging around, pushing her legs up over her head. He was always tying her spread-eagled to the bed, always rolling her onto her front, and if not onto her front, then onto her back. Other times she was pulled up by her hips and made to kneel in a kind of a bridge at the edge of the mattress. He died tragically three years later, and ever after brown-haired men made her cry.

The three young brothers knew nothing of this. They had seen nude pictures here and there, sat across from her at meals as though they'd been through things she'd never understand. They had no idea about her at all. They were naive in the way young boys are about middle-aged women who don't seem so cool.

The mother was distracted. The nurse was distracted.

The grandmother, meanwhile, insisted that Eleanor was responsible for her stroke. It was Eleanor's fault, she said, and so she stuck out her cane to trip Eleanor whenever Eleanor walked by, and pointed her chin at Eleanor. Finally the old woman locked herself in her room and complained about it to her friends over the phone; how Eleanor caused her stroke. Eleanor discussed this with the nurse. They agreed that the phone was making her excited, and so they took away the phone.

One morning many months before, the old woman had stood at the top of the stairs, clutching at her head dramatically and wailing, "I've been poisoned! I'm dying!" Then she fell down both flights and collapsed in a brittle heap in the main hallway, where she convulsed for several minutes before losing consciousness.

Tim had been the only witness to the scene, and the others grew very jealous as he described it to them later, vividly acting the whole thing out. They wished they'd seen it too. It would have been very funny.

They all went to visit the old woman in the hospital: the nurse, the boys, the boys' well-mannered mother, and Eleanor. Eleanor liked the old woman. The old woman, she felt, understood her. She regarded Eleanor as a real cheapie, which was right, Eleanor thought. After all, she had been taken, and allowed herself to be taken, and still thought about it a bit, sometimes.

Lying under the white sheets, and without moving much, the old woman pulled a notepad out from under her body.

It was her will. She passed it around. She had decided to leave everything funny to Tim.

It wasn't the first time Tim had left school feeling sullen. Walking home that afternoon he kicked the bigger stones at cars, hoping to cause some damage, even if it was only minor. Down the block men were digging up the road and dust blew into his nose and eyes. He had to keep spitting. He found the butt of a cigarette in the gutter and picked it up and wiped it off and lit it, still walking. It made him feel cruel.

"This is my life," he thought deeply and soberly. It felt as dramatic and decrepit as riding the rails. When he arrived home the nurse took off his jacket. In his room he lay on his bed under the model airplanes hanging from his ceiling and thought it again, "This is my fucking life." His curiosity returned. Was this the first time he had ever thought the word *fuck*?

Eleanor was at the door. He could feel it.

"What do you want, Eleanor?"

Eleanor apologized and wondered if she could come in, and she squeezed herself carefully through the opening, not wanting to budge the door. She looked slowly at Tim, then sat on his bed, but upon catching his expression she stood.

"What do you think of this letter?" she asked, and pulled it from the pocket of her skirt, unfolded it, and handed it to him.

He took it blithely and held it in front of his face, reading it beginning to end while Eleanor waited anxiously.

"I think he's in love with you," said Tim, handing it back.

"Really, really?" Eleanor tried not to seem excited, but she shouldn't have tried; it was useless. She had lived long enough, one would have thought, to have learned some things about herself, like that she couldn't hide her feelings. Obviously no friend had been good or wise enough to tell her.

"He loves you," Tim affirmed. He wasn't the least bit surprised. There were all sorts of pathetic and desperate people in the world, he knew that. He looked briefly at Eleanor from under his lids. It was the second time he had ever looked at her with a man's eyes. First time was when she had moved into the house, but that was just for an instant.

Eleanor began to blush. She wasn't sure whether to leave the room or not. She felt she should, but she also wanted him to say something more, something that would explain it all. Tim said nothing. He just looked.

Eleanor was very fond of ice cream. She told the man, when he called, that he would have to buy her ice cream if he wanted to take her on a date. He agreed and she dropped the receiver twice before hanging it in the cradle properly.

The next evening she sat at the little table in her room, wearing red lipstick and pinning up her hair. The old woman pushed her walker past the open door on her way to the toilet. She stopped when she saw Eleanor fancying herself up.

"Eleanor," she shouted, "are you going out with a man?"

"Yes," Eleanor said, not turning around.

The old woman thought about it, then nodded. "Good for you." She continued down the hall.

Eleanor walked out of the house and stood waiting by the front gate. The night was cool; it was only seven o'clock so it wasn't completely dark out. It was blue. The man came along the sidewalk and when he saw Eleanor he started running towards her, shouting out her name. Eleanor was delighted. He came to an abrupt stop right where she was standing and looked down at her proudly, huffing and grinning.

"I have a gift for you," he said, and held out a big box covered in wrapping paper and tied with a bow.

"Shall I open it now?" Eleanor wondered.

"Yes. No. I don't know."

"I'll wait," she decided, and hurried up the path to take the box inside. Her dress was swishing and he watched it as it moved. He watched the top of the dress as it left the house and hastened back towards him.

"Shall we go, Eleanor? Are you ready to go, Eleanor?"

His saying her name twice made her a little uneasy.

"Why not," she said.

He held her by the elbow and they walked the three blocks to the ice cream shop. It was uncomfortable for her to be held in such a way, but she didn't mind enough to say anything about it. He seemed very pleased and neither of them talked much. When they arrived at the parlour he held the door open for her. After she had picked out her flavours he

67

made her sit in one of the booths while he paid and brought over the bowls himself. He sat down across from her.

"I like to wait on you, Eleanor," he said. "You're beautiful."

"Thank you," she replied, and felt smarter and more assured than before, as though she had several other men after her tail as well. She felt removed and superior. She was content to find herself judging him.

Within a few minutes they were bent down over their bowls, eating their ice cream in silence. Then Eleanor felt a chill cover her arms and neck. She looked across the table and caught the man grinning up at her, head tilted, eyes bright.

"What is it, John?" Eleanor put down her spoon and looked around uncomfortably.

"Ah, you're just so . . ." He shook his head as if in awe, then happily went back to eating his ice cream.

This happened two more times.

As they were getting up to leave she told him it might be best if he just walked her home now. Once outside, he attempted to put his coat around her shoulders, but she told him it was unnecessary, that the coat she was wearing was fine. When they reached her gate, he held it open and stood there politely, not expecting a kiss.

"Well, I *am* pleased about the ice cream," she said with dignity, aware of herself as considerably more mature than when the evening began.

"You're welcome, Eleanor," he said, and produced that same moony smile he'd given her at the ice cream shop. She wondered if he could see through her dress.

In the house it was warm, like summer, and the lamps shed a peachy light on everything. It was the perfect house to come home to. As she hung up her coat with a weary hand, she noticed the present he had given her resting on a stand in the vestibule. She wasn't so interested in opening it now. It was as though she expected to see his grinning face winking up at her from the bottom. She lifted it and took it into the living room, sat down in a plush armchair, and rested it on her knees. She didn't usually drink, but she would have gone and poured herself some booze from the cupboard if it hadn't been for that big box in her lap. She began untying the ribbon when the boys' mother softly appeared around the edge of the doorframe.

"Oh," she said in her gentle voice. "You're back."

"Yes," Eleanor said, with slight pride. "He gave me this present."

"Well that's very romantic," said the mother. "That's *very* sweet and romantic." She looked around. "I should think."

"Do you want to open it?" Eleanor asked pointlessly, and her newfound refinement faded into mush. The boys' mother always made her feel common and awkward. She was upset. The change within her had seemed permanent, but it was nothing.

"Oh no," whispered the mother in such a light, airy voice. She was so slight; not like a bird, more like a feather. "I'll just go," she said, hesitating a little, obviously wanting to stay, but leaving anyway.

Eleanor returned to the gift. She unfolded the paper,

which was red with blue-and-yellow boats, and opened the box, first glancing away, then looking down into it. Lying at the bottom was a beanie with a visor. It was made up of six coloured wedges leading down from a button — purple, green, yellow. It was way too small for her head.

She put the lid back on the box and placed it down beside the chair, then started up the stairs to bed. She had no idea why he had given her such a ridiculous and inappropriate gift. It didn't even make her laugh.

THE ACCIDENT

There was an accident on the street yesterday. Seven cars piled up one after another, pressing into the backs of each other. When I saw it (people tell me) I put my hands to my face and I screamed. Then I passed out. As it turns out, quite a number of people who were on the street saw fit to help me — and not the people scrunched in those cars. Could be because I'm beautiful.

I have been told that I'm beautiful ever since the world first saw my face. I have considered this something of a charming feature of my personality, partly because it means that whatever else slips away, whatever else I am incapable of, I still have one thing most people don't: beauty.

When I came to, the first thing I saw was the face of a moustached man. He was wearing a hat and looking down concerned into my eyes. I blinked up at him and he lifted his face in pure joy. "She's all right!" The small crowd that had gathered about me cheered, and I was helped to my feet by another man and a lady who was older and dressed quite nicely. The lady then proceeded to brush off my suit as I stood there dazed, blinking at the world around me.

"It sure is a lucky thing you didn't hit your head when you fell," said the man with the moustache. "You could have been bleeding all through your pretty hair."

I didn't know what to say. How to thank such kind-hearted people? However I was in no condition to be polite, so I just walked away. At dinner that night, my husband told me that it was just lucky that there are kind people in this world willing to help a stranger like me.

"What's lucky, Tom," I said, "is that I'm beautiful. Those people wouldn't have helped me if I wasn't so beautiful."

"Not true," he said, shaking his head. "You're just a lucky gal to have fallen into the care of such nice people. Someone," he winked, "was looking out for you."

"Yes, the men in the street."

He furrowed his brow. Then he let me have the best portion of the meat, and I smiled because he is such a generous man, at times.

MR. JONES'S FIRST OUTING

For the past seven years Mr. Jones had been taking care of his wife who had long been sick and ended up dying. When he reentered the society of his friends and enemies he knew nothing of the world — or of what had changed and what had stayed the same — but when he saw Fritz sitting at a bar sipping on some gin, he couldn't help but say, "Fritz," and so the new times became like the old.

"Come over and sit with me, you poor bugger," said Fritz.

So Mr. Jones sat with Fritz, and Fritz put down his drink and looked into his friend's eyes and said, "Most respectfully, man, can we talk about something else now?"

"Oh yes, of course," replied Mr. Jones, and he looked down shamefully into his milk.

"Good. Y'know I was buying a comic the other day, see," but just as Fritz was getting to the good part a hag and a young woman came up to their table and stood there waiting. The young woman was tall and her breasts pressed out; she had a fine body that appealed to men. Knowing this, the hag said calmly, "Can we sit down with you? My cousin here doesn't know anyone."

"Well . . ." said Fritz, who didn't like meeting new people.

"But of course," said Mr. Jones, and he hurriedly arranged the chairs so that the doll sat in one and he sat down beside her. The girl looked around, all bright-eyed, and Mr. Jones asked her profession.

"Me?" she chirped.

"She's my friend," said the hag, smiling till her gums showed.

"I'm her friend," nodded the girl, and everyone could tell she wasn't even smarter than a crash test dummy.

"I suppose you want to talk about events in the world," sighed Fritz, with difficulty.

"No. We want to see if we can become your friends," said the hag.

"I don't know if that would be possible today," said Fritz. He hated talking to new people. One never knew how one was being evaluated.

Turning to Mr. Jones, the old hag's eyes suddenly filled with tears. She sputtered, "We heard about your horrible life and how your wife died, and truly we wanted to come over and give our compassion and support, if necessary."

"Oh, thank you," blushed Mr. Jones, looking down and all around.

"You looked like such a nice man, and I said to Janie, 'Come now dear, we have to go over and tell that man that he's a real hero' — a real hero, that's what you are." She looked hopefully into Mr. Jones's eyes and saw him avert them gently.

"Well, thank you for saying that, but I loved my wife — love my wife — loved my wife — and there's nothing heroic about love."

The hag shrugged and, bending her head in close to the table, said in a confidential tone, "She loves me too, and do you think she'd stick around if my toes were curling up?"

The dollish young woman continued to smile.

"No, it's true," said the hag, shaking her head. "She'd be off to Timbuktu with her stupid little friends. I'm a lot of fun while I'm still kicking, but my days are numbered. I know it for a fact. I've even got the number." Sitting back in her chair she pulled her chin into her neck and searched around in her pocket, pulling out a ratty piece of paper. "Ah. A hundred and eighteen."

"What?" chirped the doll.

"Nothing. Go back to your ginger ale." Then in a petty voice, "You see? You think she could nurse me back to health, or even put me to die properly? Impossible! When we go home she sits in front of the TV. When we go out she stares ahead as if we never left! I know you two think it is madness, but once in a while she's a very good lover, and that makes up for all the rest. Her friends are terrible people, though. They have no morality and look at me as though I should have put the peas in the pot years ago! When we all know it isn't true. Right? Right? You know. You were a nurse."

Mr. Jones nodded.

"So anyway," said the hag, leaning back. She sighed and looked around. "I'm bored, eh, doll?"

The young woman smiled, her teeth shining brightly. She was no longer so appealing to the men, now that they had talked in confidence with the hag.

"So . . ." said Fritz. "How much longer are you going to stay at this table?"

Mr. Jones said quickly, "My friend is shy and people he doesn't know make him nervous."

"No reason to be nervous," said the hag. "If you knew us you'd see that there's nothing to be intimidated by, and far from being better than you, we're actually less or the same."

"Is it true?" asked Fritz suddenly, and Mr. Jones felt disgusted with the turn in the conversation. Was this the sort of tedious insecurity the world had come to?

"Don't you realize that in general about people?" said the hag. "We're nothing! Not at all! Not a thing!"

"But I always assume," continued Fritz, with interest, "that people are better than me, and are judging me with a divine right."

"Let's go," said the hag swiftly, and she rushed the young woman deep into the smoky bar.

"Wait!" cried Fritz, standing up.

Mr. Jones turned to look at his friend, whose face was now red and desperate. "I don't know if it solves anything," said Mr. Jones, choosing his words carefully. "After all, you never know what she might have meant. One can never know. And even if you do know, it might not even be true."

"Oh, go back to your apartment!" spat Fritz, and he twisted his body and bounded off with his drink in hand, after the hag and the doll.

Now Mr. Jones was all alone. He should never have gone out if this was the sort of behaviour one encountered in the world. He missed the past; the quiet nothingness of lying in bed next to his dying wife, stroking her wet hair as she breathed with difficulty, and opened her eyes somewhat, every few days. Those were gentle times; how the light came through the window, how he barely slept at all, and how she lived with pain.

A Few Adventures
of the Young Fornicator

The landlord had been seeking rent from the young fornicator for two weeks now. Every time he knocked on the door
there would be sounds, then no sounds. The landlord was
furious and his wife slapped him. This caused the landlord to
prowl the yard, the floor of the young fornicator, and the
main lobby. Still, the fornicator managed to elude him, and
the landlord's wife yelled at him for things relating to their
life together and to the building and to their daughter Beth's
birthday.

At sixteen Beth had been a little too bony, but at eighteen
she had fine breasts and the kind of stomach that young
women with large stomachs longed for, and she was dating
three boys from her college.

It was the young fornicator's day off and he lay in bed with
a girl. Her hair was long and she was twisting it around her

finger when suddenly he stood and went to look out the open window. He began to tell a story.

"I've seen the landlord's daughter before, but she's always had this vapid expression, so naturally I thought she was a little stupid. But then I was in the park one day and she was sitting on a bench, when this kid with lots of allergies went up to her."

"Where are you going with this?" the girl asked, alert and possessive at the suggestion of another woman.

"I don't know." The young fornicator returned from the window. Somewhere in the telling the story had gotten lost. He did not know where it had gone. The girl insisted they fool around some more and so they did, though the young man was not so engaged; his mind was resting on the landlord's daughter.

Beth was standing on the corner in the hot sun waiting for the bus, and she had been waiting a long time. There was sweat under her arms. The young fornicator came walking down the street. She recognized him from her father's building. He mumbled out a hello and sat on the back of a bench and watched her, but she did not respond. There were too many men she was seeing already.

The young fornicator cleared his throat, then asked a question.

"What?" she said, irritated. He spoke so quietly!

"Nothing," he mumbled. This did not impress her and she spat out, "Today is my birthday and my father forgot to get me a cake. What a jerk! Do you know what this means to me? I was expecting a nice blue one: blue icing on the outside with chocolate on the inside! Such a jerk."

The young fornicator did not know what to say to this. The bus came and Beth got on. The young man walked back to his apartment.

In his bed he found a friend of his mother's. He went and stood at the window and lit a cigarette. She looked at him with red eyes.

"I suppose you only think of me as your mother's friend. Is that why you won't sleep with me? I'm young still!" His mother's friend burst into fresh tears and buried her head in the pillow, heaving. He blew out smoke. He was tired of these women. Let the landlord collect his rent. Within half an hour he had shuffled the old woman out of there and sat down on his couch awaiting the landlord's knock. Sure enough the knock came and he opened the door and there was the landlord with a furious look on his face and a frying pan quivering in his hand.

"I want my rent! Where have you been since the first?"

The young fornicator invited the landlord in and made him stand by the window as he looked through his coat pockets, trying to find his wallet. As he approached the landlord with the money, the sudden bright light of the sun beamed down upon the landlord, and in that instant the landlord looked so much like his daughter that the fornicator felt the pull.

"Give it to me," the landlord said, and the young man

allowed the bills to be snatched from his hand, and saw, over the landlord's shoulder, young Beth coming up the driveway to the tall white-rise.

"Your daughter is here," the fornicator said.

The landlord turned to look out the window. He put the bills in his pocket. She was carrying in her hand a bag, and in the bag was a box, and in the box was a chocolate cake with shiny blue icing.

WHAT CHANGED

After all, they were a man and a woman. There was no reason for them not to fall in love.

When the man fell, the woman fell, and when the woman fell, the man fell. It is hard to say now who fell first.

As they were falling, other things happened in other places, but where they were it was just he for she and she for he, and that very night they went out for pasta.

They could barely order, which irritated the waitress, but it was only because they were so much in love, and so leaning over the table, and so fondling each other's hands, and so fondling each other's arms, and so staring into each other's eyes, and so smiling dopily.

They were doped. Or they were falling in love.

He said, "Come away with me this weekend. I must have you and only you and no one else around."

And she said, "Oh that's a fantastic idea. Let's do it."

So their attention shifted from each other's face and hands on to where they would go, where they would stay, how they would get there, what he had to clear up first, what she'd tell her family.

That night they kissed passionately on the front porch of her parents' house, but she went inside alone. And she thought of him when he was not there, and he thought of her when she was not there as well.

When the weekend came he picked her up in his car and they drove east down the highway, and she giggled and laughed, and he just laughed, and she squirmed in her seat and tried to touch his body, and their bags were in the back, and the sun was out, and the windows were open, and she sang songs that were playing on the radio, and she was so joyful and he was damn happy.

They made a stop to get some lunch and kissed each other's lips and tongues right outside the restaurant. She kept her eyes open to see who was looking, and he kept his hands on her.

Back in the car she felt sleepy, so they stopped again to get her a coffee so she would not fall asleep, so they would not miss a moment of their weekend together.

When they arrived at the place where they were headed, she sat in the car and looked around while he got a key from the concierge, and he picked up the luggage, and she carried the fragile wine bottles. Together they hiked down a path through the trees and she said to him, "Have you been here before?"

And he said, "No. My brother told me about it."

And she was happy, and he felt okay too, and though the

lie was unnecessary, it made things better.

That night they got drunk and did all those things, and in the morning they got up and did all those things. As he was cooking breakfast with the groceries they had brought, she called out from the bed, "I think we'll never fight. I could never see fighting with you."

And he called back over his shoulder, "You could never make me mad."

She wiggled gleefully into the covers, and he felt a loving rise at her high and musical voice.

In the afternoon they went for a swim, and, swimming, he tried to pull off her bathing suit, but she coquettishly swam away, batting her arms and legs at him. She called, "Keep away, you madman! I'm being raped by a madman!"

And while this initially jarred him, he quickly relaxed and decided he liked her impetuous thoughtless ways.

In the evening he made a fire, and everything was perfect and had been going perfectly, and she lay back in his arms and thought, It's picture perfect. It's just like we're in a movie. And she said to him, "Doesn't it feel like we're in a movie? In some made-up fantasy land?"

And he said, "Mmmm," and kissed the top of her head, and it was even more like a movie, like everything she had seen and heard about love, and she was involved, and it was with him.

She said, "I wish this weekend would never end."

And when she said that, in a way, it made his arms just clutch her tighter, and her face withdrew into thinking about

Monday, and the ride home, which would be worse, and he felt her thinking, and he started thinking too.

She tried to brush it off, to cover it up, as if she hadn't said it, as if it wasn't true at all, that of course they would be at that cabin forever, and she said to him, to make it all better, "Truly, it's like a dream."

But it wasn't like a dream. Not really. And they got drunk and did all that and fell asleep, and when they woke in the morning she felt crummy and he grew irritated.

Because he had to pack their bags and clean up everything while she lay in bed just watching him. She had said, "Just let me watch you. I just want to watch you." And he had said, "Well, you're watching me," in a joking sort of way, but he did not want to be watched. He wanted to be helped. And she flopped back into the pillows, into the covers, and she said, "I wish we could stay forever." And she said, "You take the first shower. I can't get up."

So he did.

While she was in her shower he opened the door and stood there watching, but she cried, "Get out!" And though she was joking, sort of, she really did need her privacy in the mornings, especially in the bathroom, so he left to pack the car.

"One last swim?" he asked when she emerged, drying her hair with a towel. And she said, "No, the water will be too cold."

She said, "I'll make you breakfast. Sit down."

And she made them cereal with bananas cut into it, and

she apologized, laughing, saying, "I don't know how to cook." Yesterday he had made her gourmet omelettes with salad and juice and had squeezed the oranges with his own bare hands. She just opened the box and poured in the milk. But the bananas were a nice gourmet touch.

He said, "It's one o'clock." And she said, "I never want to leave." And they took one last long look at the cabin, so as never to forget it, and they walked out to the car, him leading the way.

The ride home took five hours, and she lay back in her seat and looked out the window, and the sky was dark and wet, and he was tired, and he kept his eyes on the road, and they talked little, and when they did it was only to reminisce about Saturday.

As they were driving into the city, she said mournfully, "I hate this city. I hate my job. And I don't want to go back to my parents."

And he said, "I have a damn early morning meeting tomorrow and I have so much work to catch up on." And he said, "We shouldn't have gone."

But he didn't mean it that way.

When they got to her house, he unloaded the bags and carried them to the door and dropped them on the stoop, and they stood there looking at each other, but he seemed impatient. And she made her eyes both melancholy and bright, and said, "I had such a wonderful weekend. Thanks."

And he said, "I did too."

And he said, "I'll give you a ring tomorrow."

And he thought about the work he had at home, and she thought about her parents sitting around the table and how she'd have to talk to them, and they kissed, and he went back to his car, and as she was unlocking the door, he drove off and away.

JANIS AND MARCUS

There was condensation on the windowpane.

"The philanthropists will continue their verbal and written exposition," Marcus noted wearily, not speaking into the receiver as he put down the phone. Janis, on the other end, hung up hard. She hated when he would talk to his cat.

Now it was just one of those sunny days when everyone was outside being happy. There were strollers on the streets and babies clenching their fists at each other, dogs sniffing each other up and down, and mothers stopping to chat with cool drinks in their hands, rich with caffeine and sunglasses on.

Janis and Marcus were sitting in the park, watching the kids on a jungle gym. Marcus was saying, "In a word, the sole means that will be employed by the philanthropists will be exposition; and the sole object that they will propose in their expositions will be that of inducing kings to use their powers to bring about the political changes that have become necessary."

Janis was watching the children play. Not even turning her head she said, "Some years ago I accompanied a candidate for the presidency on his campaign tour. He was, like all such rascals, an amusing fellow, and I came to like him very much."

That evening they drank Chartreuse under the stars, and Janis's roommate joined them with a glass of lemonade on the porch, overlooking the apartment parking lot.

"I had a terrible day," said the roommate. "I was doing the laundry since morning. Can you believe it?"

"Yes I can," said Janis, "because you have no sense of real beauty. You always miss the glorious days to do chores."

"But I *do* have a sense of real beauty," her roommate said, "which is apparent because of my despair at missing a day such as today."

"Then why didn't you put off the laundry till tomorrow?"

Her roommate shrugged. "Why do birds fly?"

"Because it's their nature."

"I don't want to get into one of these discussions," her roommate said, putting down the lemonade and pinning up her hair.

"You see," said Janis. "You intentionally miss everything. That's the problem with you."

Marcus was getting a headache. He had been thinking about nothing before the roommate came out. Now he was thinking about everything.

"I have to go," he said, rising.

"No, don't go! We're not fighting."

"You know me," Marcus said kindly. "I like to be alone." He kissed Janis on the head and let himself out the door as Janis watched him leave.

"See what you've done?" she asked her roommate.

"Don't blame me," her roommate said.

Janis sighed. If only she made enough money she would live alone.

THE RASPBERRY BUSH

A little old woman who never stopped smiling walked into her kitchen from her garden. She had been standing in the sun for twenty minutes, tears in her eyes, looking at her beautiful raspberry bush that had died overnight. Instead of perky red raspberries she had found them black and brittle, and they fell to the ground at the slightest touch.

The sun shone through the kitchen window and lit up everything with sparkles of gold as the little old woman who never stopped smiling called up her sister in such a sorrow. Her sister was eighty-eight and lived in California. She said into the phone, "The raspberries are dead."

Her sister replied, "Well, the grandchildren are flunking out of school and Martha is pregnant and Sam is divorcing his wife and his wife is taking up with a gypsy girl. The infant has the flu and she never stops coughing. I was over there the other day and all they talk about is money ever since Tom got fired from the plant. Not to mention that Timothy never stops dating and we all think he has AIDS or gonorrhea or something. The news, I saw it today, told about a hurricane in the Andes which, as you know, is where David and Sue went skiing last week. Everyone here is miserable with grief and worry."

The little old woman listened to her sister, and when she had finished the little old woman who never stopped smiling put down the phone and sat in her kitchen that was dotted with gold.

There was a knock.

"Hello?" called the woman, and she stood up and padded to the door and peeped through the peephole and saw a young man in a delivery cap holding a bouquet of flowers. She opened the door.

"Why," her lips curled up in a smile. "These can't be for me."

"Are you Miss Marcia —"

"No, young man. She's next door." And the little old woman who never stopped smiling closed the door and went to sit at her kitchen table. The day was long; there were eight more hours in it. She had planned to eat the raspberries, one by one, every last one of them. But overnight the bush had died and there wouldn't be raspberries ever again.

The little old woman laid down her head and started to cry. She cried at her table every day, but no one knew it.

FRAMES FROM CHRISTIANITY

Recently the man had been asking questions. He had taken to walking the streets at night, an old scarf wound tightly around his mouth and ears, a satchel in hand full of books. He would stop to chat with people, especially the prostitutes. Before this spurt of questions the man had never spoken to a prostitute, though a person he knew had slept with one once.

It was a Thursday evening and the man put on his endless scarf and made his way down la rue Hébert, a nice residential street with a large empty parking lot. He arrived in the lot at seven-thirty but none of the prostitutes were there, so he sat on a pylon and waited, asking himself, "Why did I bring all these books? I always carry around too many books and I never even read any." The man had been well-educated once and during that time had read a great many books. But lately he had been asking questions and reading all of nothing.

Miss Moriarty entered the lot wearing a green feathered hat and carrying a red purse. She looked just like a holiday.

The man jumped up and threw an arm in the air, happily crying, "Miss Moriarty!"

She glanced around to see who it was. When she spotted the man she approached him with a disinterested look, seeming edgy. She did not like this man, but the man, who proceeded to pull his scarf down to just below his chin, liked everyone.

"Where are the other ladies?" he asked. "And why are you the first one here?"

She said she didn't know and didn't care. Then she left to prowl the lot. He wasn't sure what she was looking for, and as she wasn't either, she again wound up beside him.

"I'm so sick of this lot." Her voice was dry. "I must have been coming here for five years. There must be better places to go. Do you know of any better places?"

"For what, Miss Moriarty?"

"Oh, I don't know. Do you have a chocolate bar?"

The man checked his pocket and his bag but all he had were too many books and two dollars. This caused them to start off towards the nearest convenience store. As they walked down the street, she looked in his dictionary.

"Misanthrope," she said. "Miscreant. Molehill. Mansion. Molar. Moose."

"Yes, that dictionary you are holding has every word you could ever need," the man said proudly, and what he didn't say but what he implied was "and it's mine."

"I don't like dictionaries," she said. They were only a block from the store and the street was dark. Raccoons scratched their nails on the trees as they passed. "I don't even like *people* with dictionaries," she said, and gave it back to him. He frowned and put it in his bag.

"Are you *sure* you don't like people with dictionaries?" he asked, giving her a second chance. He no longer felt like spending two dollars on her.

"I'm sure," she said.

In the little grocery store she picked out a terrible chocolate bar with caramel and mint. While paying for it the man bought a weekly lottery ticket. "If I win this you get half," he told her.

She left the store before him. Turning towards the lot she flung her hair, and her lips were almost fluorescent under the streetlight. "Quit following me," she said. "Go home."

He stood and watched silently as she walked away. He ripped the lottery ticket in two and dropped it in the gutter.

That night in bed the man sat with his dictionary on his lap, moving slowly through the pages with tenderness and care, as if it were a family photo album. His face showed a wistful, almost curious nostalgia.

When he woke in the morning he arranged his hair into its proper place and put on his shoes and left. He went to call on his uncle Charlie, who had an unlisted number.

The two men sat near Uncle Charlie's window and the man kept his coat and scarf on. They ate ice cream from bowls. He asked Uncle Charlie about the old days, but Charlie said, "It's a secret," and wouldn't tell him anything.

"Why are you dressed like that?" Charlie asked.

"Because I'm cold."

When the man left, his uncle bent towards the window to see his nephew walk down the path, but as he didn't see anyone leave, he soon fell asleep under a patchwork comforter.

That afternoon, the man who had been asking questions ran out of things to do. He sat himself below a tree that was planted by the side of the road and idly watched the wildlife — squirrels, chipmunks, babies. He was soon kicked off the lawn. He hadn't realized it was private property.

"Why don't you just go on home?" he was asked by the property-owner.

"Why *don't* I just go on home?" he asked himself, sour. "Is going home such a failure?" he asked himself again.

A BENCH FOR
MARIANNE AND TODD

Marianne walked the edge of the pier and looked down and saw her reflection staring back at her. It was an ugly reflection, one she had gotten used to, and it stared back at her dully. She spat into the water, perverting it, and walked back to the sand. There sat her first and last boyfriend, Todd, a big guy with red hair and nothing much going for him except his exacting kindness.

She sat down beside him and dumped a handful of sand between his legs.

"Hey!" he said, a little bit miffed. Then softer, joking, "That feels kind of funny."

"Oh Todd," she said, and thought about her ugliness and thought about Todd's ugliness and said, "We're both filthy, ugly, unattractive people. There are people much more beautiful than us, with better lives than us, and then there's you and me, you my only love, and me your only love, and we're what's left of the rest. We're the refuse of humanity and here we are on the coldest day of the year, alone in the sand, looking out over the water, and we're totally totally miserable."

Todd thought about what she had said, disagreed with some of it, and looked at her face, which was looking out over the sea, and he said, "Don't worry. We don't need anybody else. I have you and you have me, and even if we are two very ugly people with no hopes or ambitions, we have each other, and nobody else has that."

Marianne considered it a moment, disagreed with some of it and agreed with the other parts, thought of turning her head and giving him a kiss, but decided against it. She thought, "I don't need to prove anything," and she felt the pimple festering under the skin of her nose throb a little.

She said, "But don't you see? That makes us nothing in the eyes of the world. So you have me and I have you. So what? We're just a couple of dumb animals, ugly dumb animals, and nobody loves us, and nobody looks at us, but when they do they shudder. That matters more than any paltry love we have."

She lay back on the cold wet sand, felt her hair tangle with the stones, and looked up at the dark grey sky.

Todd leaned back on his hands, looked farther over the waves, and felt small and lowly, like the only man in the world, which made him feel bigger but lonely, and yet he didn't touch her hand, he didn't need to pretend. He yawned, though he wasn't tired, and yawned again, though he wasn't bored, and said, "Let's walk," but she said no.

Ten minutes passed, then another five, and neither of them spoke. Their thoughts were hazy, somewhat around their loneliness and ugliness, and finally Marianne said, "Whatever you want," and they got up and started to walk down the boardwalk, on which no one else was walking, and Marianne said, "Where are all the people?"

And Todd said, "At home, in front of their fireplaces, wine in hand, love by their side, all warm and happy and beautiful, like you know."

And Marianne said, "Why are we the only ones here?"

And Todd said, "There's nowhere else for us to go."

Later, Marianne sighed, and Todd asked, "Are you crying?"

And Marianne said, "No."

"Todd," said Marianne, "are we ever going to get married and have children?"

And Todd said, "I don't think so."

And they both felt something.

"Todd," said Marianne, "I love you. I really do."

And Todd said, "You're a silly girl, but I love you too."

They didn't take each other's hand. They sat down on a bench and looked out over the water and heard not the rustle of people or the roar of traffic or the raindrops on the lake. They didn't hear each other breathing, or feel the presence of God. They heard their heavy thoughts and slumped back on the bench and contemplated some.

Well, if it wasn't the sea, so dark and grim. If it wasn't the sky, the worst of the year. If it wasn't the weather, the coldest day yet. And everyone inside escaping it. And there they were, ugly and forlorn, in a day just as ugly and just as forlorn, but still a day, still a day.

THE POET AND THE NOVELIST
AS ROOMMATES

The poet went softly to the novelist's bedroom, while the novelist lay asleep, sleep coming out heavy like a stink through his nose. The poet stood in the doorway, watching, pressing down on the doorframe.

He loved his roommate. But not like that. It was four in the morning and why had he woken? Sleep was a burden for a man like him. And yet here was a man who slept through the night.

"He must be in a state of guilt," the poet thought, before turning and going to bed. Padding through the hall he asked himself quietly, "What am I doing in this city? Even looking at the clouds I feel I have lost my imagination."

On the woman's first day at work the poet helped her with her boxes, but as he was helping he was looking away.

"Do you know this is my seventieth sick day since I started here?" he asked.

"But you're here," she said.

"Yes, I know." And he went to the bathroom and peed blood.

When he returned she was sitting upright, typing at her computer like a good girl. There was a calculated grace about her and it was this that caused him, eyes drooping and weary, to lean over the partition and say to her face, "Come with me after work. I will show you a good place to drink around here."

"I'll come, sure," she said, looking up, and there was no guile expressed, just a big round smile and those hateful eyes that only women understood.

When the workday ended he took her by the arm and led her to The Poodle, which was seedy and disreputable and no place for a woman from a cubicle to be. He looked around. She was wearing a bra on tight beneath her clothing.

"Sit down here at this booth," he said, pushing in her body with both his hands, "and I will get you a soda water."

"I take gin in my soda water," she said hopefully, and the poet walked away with a shudder. These modern women. They had no sense of their own indecency.

When he returned with the drinks he slipped into the booth and began to twitch in boredom as he listened to her story.

"I have a husband and three children," she began.

"But you look eighteen," he said mournfully, and swished his drink. A husband and three children. "You should not be dressed like that then," he concluded.

She furrowed her brow and sucked up her drink with pristine fury. "Thank you for this," she said, smacking down the glass and dropping the straw from her lips as she walked.

When he returned that night he found his roommate working on his novel. Looking up from the computer his roommate beckoned him over.

"I think there is a bug behind the glass," said the novelist, pointing to a place on the screen, then tracing it, following it.

"I don't see it," the poet replied, eyes crossed in intoxication.

"Go to bed," the novelist said, and the poet did.

When the poet woke he remembered the woman, the one with the husband and the three lovely kids. Probably right now she was frantically diapering them, or shoving sandwiches into their boxes, not thinking anything, just scurrying around with a phone in her chin, talking to her sister in Ottawa.

"It has been so in politics, it has been so in religion, and it has been so in every other department of human thought," he thought, and got up and undressed and went to the shower and rubbed himself hard, and went to his room where he dressed in brown and walked in the rain to work.

When he arrived the woman in the cubicle was already there. Her spine was haughty and tense and she was turned away. But as he sat and arranged his folders he knew that she was thinking of him. "She can't do any better than me," he determined. Yes, he would destroy her. This woman with the husband and the three lovely kids: she was looking for an affair, a real sweaty romance, he could smell it on her skin.

Indeed, by the coffeemaker at eleven a.m. she said, "I would like to go home with you tonight. I would like to see where you live."

"It is not a sight for a lady," he said, dangling this info in front of her. "It's a small place. A man's place. I'm a poet, you see, and I live there alone with my roommate of seven years who is cruel. Women fall in love with him but he cannot love them back. He is a novelist. He's very messy."

"I want to come home with you," the woman said, pressing her eyes into him and spilling the coffee.

That night they sat around the table: the poet, the novelist, and the woman from the cubicle. The woman from the cubicle, eyes all alight, looked back and forth from one to the other. One was so gruff and silent and thick, like a real man! and the other was disinterested and distracted and edgy, like a real man! She was falling in love with them both.

The novelist, feeling violated for reasons he could not understand, got up and left the table and went to his computer and peered in, and again saw the bug behind the screen. "Damn it!" he cried, pounding his fist into his desk. The poet looked dreary and did not respond.

The woman said, "Please, tell me about your life. You must be fascinating. I have never known a poet before, except for one in high school. And I don't even know if he's still a poet."

The poet said darkly, "Don't tell me that." Then, "Come

106

with me to the bedroom. It is my bedroom and I should like to show it to you."

The woman put down her fork and followed in behind. She was delighted. She felt so bohemian. She wanted to take off all her clothes.

"Good," he said, turning on a lamp. "You can see now on my wall two letters from Al Purdy, telling me I am good but not good enough."

He sat on the bed which was low to the floor and spread apart his legs and looked up at her as she walked around the narrow space, fingering all the things.

"That is a picture taken of me when I was in Poland. I was a professor."

"You look very Polish here."

"I know."

He lay his back on his bed and looked up at the ceiling, hands adjusted behind his head. "Do you smoke?" he asked.

"No."

"Please go into the next room and get a cigarette from my novelist roommate. He should have a pack beside him on the desk. Tell him it is for me; he will understand. If he refuses to give you one or throws a fit, leave the room at once. Sometimes it bothers him to be interrupted while writing."

The woman left the room and walked down the hall and saw the novelist hunched before his computer, deep in his chair, pressing his fingers to the screen. "Come," he said, when he heard her approach, and she moved towards his desk and placed her hands upon it and leaned archingly forward. He put one hand on her ass, felt it shifting beneath her dress.

"Do you see a bug?"

She held her breath, did not move. Then she looked evasively away and said, "I have come here to get a cigarette for the poet. He says you'll understand."

"Sure I understand." He sombrely pulled two cigarettes from the pack and she took them. She left the room and walked numbly through the hall towards the poet, and on the walk she remembered a dream. "I dreamed once I was in a room with other people."

When the poet saw her he sat upright on the bed. "Close the door," he said. "The novelist gets very jealous."

She closed the door and sat down beside him. She put the cigarettes in his hand. He looked down at them dumbly. She wanted him to throw his leg across her, push her down on the bed, slap her and rape her hard.

"Two," he said. "He must like you."

"Yes. He touched me on my bum."

"Let me see."

She lay down on her stomach and he examined her through her dress.

THE SORT OF WOMAN
FREEMAN LOVED

Freeman took the woman with the good body and drove and drove in his squat yellow car all the way to a country parish where he married her. Though she seemed at the time to be smiling, if he had looked closely he would have seen a trace of exasperation.

They settled in Manshire, where she told him, on their first day together in their brand-new house, that she was bored already and if he couldn't provide her with entertainment she'd be forced to run away. Her name was Sally. There were silly little dreams Sally had that she mistook for grand possibilities; this was her central failing.

One Saturday morning in June, the newlyweds had been living in their dreary little bungalow for three months when a salesman came to their door and introduced himself as Eli. It was his job, he said, to give people the one thing they really needed. After all, he wouldn't be much of a salesman if he gave people the one thing they really didn't want.

Ha ha. And so what was it that he could provide them with? He would be happy to open his briefcase on their living-room table and show them what a decent honest man he was. See? No gimmicks.

Well, Sally looked at Freeman and Freeman looked at Sally. He shrugged. She told him emphatically that what they needed was someone to entertain her; indeed, she began to describe the man she was thinking of in glorious detail, triple-X detail, leaving out the measurements that didn't count, like the circumference of his anus. But his eyes had to be icy blue. He ought never to smile and should have big burly hands which he never — or rarely — used in big burly ways. His skin would have to be the colour of taffy and his lips lighter than his skin. Hair curled just so.

"I can do that," the salesman said, snapping closed his briefcase. He left their house with a parting wave and a big broad smile, then turned to face the road. Locking the door behind him, the two went to sit on the couch. Sally fantasized about her elaborate dream, part of which involved making it in the role of public celebrity. Freeman smiled into her face. She was beautiful. Whatever, she was the woman he wanted.

Suddenly Sally turned to him. "You *do* know that I love you, Freeman."

Freeman smiled and nodded. He knew. She had married him and now she was living with him. She was living with him in their very own house.

The next week the salesman was back at their door with

a large wooden crate. It was a Sunday morning and since only religious good could come on a Sunday, the salesman told them that it might be best if they didn't open the package till midnight. Just out of respect for the Lord; they understood his reasoning. Could he have his money now? The salesman stood there tapping his foot and grimacing at the cloudy sky as Freeman wrote a cheque for seven thousand dollars, then softly closed the door.

In the living room his wife was already pulling nails out of the crate.

"But, but Sally, didn't you hear the man? He said it was best to leave the day to its religious duty."

"Shut up Freeman."

The crate flung open and standing there before her was the man she had ordered, exact. He was wearing thin black underwear and his arms were hanging at his sides. His face showed no expression. Sally threw her head back and laughed and hooted in glee. It was the first time Freeman had ever seen her genuinely excited and he was scared. He hurried into the kitchen and telephoned his mother.

"Sally's crazy, Mom!" he whispered into the phone, half a mile away from tears. "Mother? Mother?"

His mother was a tiny shrugging woman in a little house far away, and her words were coming faintly over the line like a whisper on a thread, so that it suddenly occurred to Freeman that she might soon be dead. Who needed this house in Manshire when there was a perfectly good house in Jackson! His mother was dying and needed to be taken care of in her little blue room! He hung up the phone and ran from the kitchen.

"Sally, we must get back to Jackson!" he cried. "I just talked to my mother and I think she might be dying! Come on now, pack your things."

Sally snapped him a horrible face. She had been standing there gleefully running her hands up and down the chest of this entertaining man, pressing her body into him, eyes all aglow. "You go," she scowled. "I don't give a shit about your boring old mother. I've got big plans."

"Oh Sally," Freeman sighed. He looked at her with a husband's sadness. "You know you can bring it with us if you want." Then he hesitantly stepped forward and held out his hand to the entertaining man. "I'm Freeman," he said, enunciating his words as though it were deaf. The doll looked blank. Freeman turned to Sally and put his hands on her shoulders. She was frail and her shoulders bent a little.

"Sally, come on now, I know you don't want to see my mother die. We have to go, this afternoon, in the car."

"Fine," she said. "But I have to get him some clothes first. We're going into town. We'll be back around three." And she took the entertaining man by the hand and walked him, like a toddler, into the road.

Freeman stood in the doorway and watched them. It was as though they had been blessed with a two-hundred-pound baby. His lips twitched once before he closed the door and went inside and started packing.

When Sally and the entertaining man returned later that afternoon they had a lot of bags, maybe about thirty, and many of them contained sequined dresses and high-heeled shoes. Freeman also noticed that Sally had gone to the hair-stylist and that her fingernails were now red. When she passed him in the hall she did so with her nose in a snub, and she didn't want to answer any questions. The entertaining man was dressed up nicely but his eyes refused to dilate.

They drove down the highway in the squat yellow car, Freeman in the front, the entertaining man and Sally in the back. She kept her arm around him. When they were about two hours from Jackson, Freeman folded down the roof and the air began gusting at them and Sally began to shriek, "My hair! My hair! You bastard! You animal!" And so Freeman hurriedly closed up the roof and drove on, accelerating. The sun was setting behind them in the west and everything was pink. Sally began talking to her man in whispers.

As soon as they arrived in Jackson, Freeman rushed through the door into his mother's house.

He found her lying in bed, shrunken into a pale skeleton. It was as though there was a little something inside her clutching at her skin, trying to pull it through her bones. Freeman collapsed. Kneeling on the rug beside the bed, he covered her face in tears and kisses, pulled on her hands, and looked into her eyes. His mother's expression did not change.

"Get in here with me, Freeman," she said, and so

Freeman got up and put his warm body under the covers with her and cuddled and held her in his arms. He cried some salty tears while she barely breathed, then she fell asleep.

Freeman tenderly arranged her hair and left the room, closing the door with a slow respectful turn of the handle. He went down the hall to his childhood room and there he found his wife sitting on the bed with the entertaining man in front of her. She was dressed in high heels and panties, and she was taking off his clothes, yanking his pants down over his thighs. Freeman stood at the door, barely able to see because of the tears that were caught in his eyes, but he could smell the nudity.

"Oh, get lost Freeman," his wife said.

Freeman closed the door and went downstairs, into the den, and lay on the couch. A fluffy little white dog ran into the room. He didn't know his mother had bought a dog. It had a bell on underneath its chin and it jumped on the couch and ran across Freeman's chest and began licking at his neck. It had the brightest, most enthusiastic eyes Freeman had ever seen, and Freeman laughed.

Suddenly Freeman heard a dull tone and with a start he jerked and bounded up the stairs. The little dog followed one step at a time.

"Mother!" he cried, but stopped before her room. Standing in the doorway was Sally, her eyes wide and frightened, and the entertaining man, holding her hand, his eyes wide and frightened too. She tugged on his arm, then he tugged on her arm, then she tugged on his. They looked no more than six years old; a brother and sister at the zoo.

THE NIGHT OF RORY

The man with the wide shoulders and the thin nose turned
left down the street. The night was cold on his face and he
put his hands in the pockets of his jacket and walked to
where the men would be; playing chess in the back of the
store, the lights too bright, the smoke too thick, and he
would be served the drink he wanted. Nobody had called
him by name all week, and in a hundred years there wouldn't
be his wife or him or anyone he knew. At one point there
were healthy Roman citizens looking up at the sky, and then
there was him and one day no one.

One block away and already he could see the terrible
sign, a white fluorescent. All he wanted was maybe two or
three drinks but not to spend the night. At home his wife
asked too many questions and talked too fast. He pushed
open the door and the place was lit up like a gymnasium.
The historian was playing chess with a critic while a colum-
nist looked on, and the man went right to the back and sat
with them, their cigarettes dangling from their mouths like
dicks. One man looked up mildly.

"Rory."

That was that. The man said "rye" and the server walked away and behind the server was a woman in a red dress. She went to the bar and stood up straight, looking over at him. He kept his eyes on the chess game. The drink came. He drank it down and still he kept his eyes on the game.

In a moment he finished and said good-bye, then ducked out past the woman into the street where the air was biting and his cheeks, only halfway down the block, were already pink and cool. In an instant the whole world could be gone and not in a way that anyone knew anything about. Couples were emerging from doorways into the night. It was the hour when people strolled and the sky was blue and you could still see the sky. He heard a clip-clopping behind him. Stopping at a light he turned and the woman halted, suddenly looking down and pressing her hands over the fronts of her thighs.

"You shouldn't have left when I came just for you."

"Why not?" he said, but he knew why; because she had come just for him. His eyes were watering from the stench of her perfume, and the beautiful couple he had seen that morning with the smiling baby might lose their baby the next day in an accident and everything in their world would just be shattered, and here she was pulling on his arm, and she had no choice either.

The light changed and he turned to face the street. He thought, "I could plough myself into that windshield and they'd all be dead, the car overturned and five people dead."

Or maybe the beautiful couple with the baby would be fine the next day but six years down the road the baby would be snatched away or run over by a car and that would be the end of their happiness forever; everything changed and no reason for it.

She caught up with him now. He had crossed without even knowing it.

"Come with me please. I don't want to be alone."

He didn't feel like going to her apartment. He avoided women but now he was following her to a neighbourhood he hardly knew, dirty with immigrants and bicycles. Now he had her figured out. Twice she turned nervously to point out places where she liked to eat but he was not impressed. He said nothing, just kept his eyes open.

She turned the lock in a door beside a bakery and he was walking up the narrow staircase before her. She had been anxious and let him up first, and the stairwell was dark and there was one blue light burning dimly at the top. When they reached the landing there were three doors and she squeezed around him and opened one up. The apartment had been done over in an oriental fashion. There were fans and umbrellas and colourful little china dolls and pillows printed with dragons and tiny orange fish in a big round bowl; he didn't care. There was nothing about anything that seemed to him real and even when he fell on the couch it sunk with his body and she was lit up by a plastic orb that glowed. She went over to the window that was big and without curtains and leaned on the sill facing him. Haloed around her head and the top of her body were the lights from the night: airplanes with flashing blue and red signals zipping through the sky, other things spinning; a moon, a planet, bright stars. His eyes blurred thick and dizzy before the hairs that were tangled like wire and fur.

The Man from Out of Town

Since his first day in town the man had been looking for a nice girl to spend good times with, but none of the girls would have him. He wasn't sure why but suspected it had to do with his status. The waitress who served him corroborated this when she called him a bum, even though he was not living on the street and he had two suits.

Not until his roommate found out the cause of his sorrowful mood did he call up a girl he had known from the park and invite her over for a dinner of pork and mashed potatoes with nutmeg.

It was her high ass that mysteriously lifted itself to her waist that caused the man to see what a nice girl she was, and how pleasant she would be to spend good times with. She also had a sweet smile and some pretty funny things to say, and whenever she laughed the sun would stream a last dying ray in through the window. Noticing all this the roommate kept playing good tunes, and by the end of the night the man and the girl were dancing together and she was laughing into his shoulder — a good sign.

In the morning she sat on his couch in a denim shirt and yesterday's underwear, and her voice seemed deep when she said, "I'm going to be late for work."

"It's Sunday though."

"Still," and she looked out the window and the greyness of the day convinced her. Wandering into his room she found her suit and zipped it up and left his apartment with a good-bye shrug. Following her with his eyes as she walked to the bus stop, the man knew that this was not the girl who would be agreeable to spending good times with him. It was not easy to explain.

In the afternoon he walked down the boardwalk, drinking warm soda from a red-and-white cup that was waxy on the outside and gradually melting, when a man with a dog caught up to him and threw his arm around his shoulder and asked in a jaunty voice what the matter was.

The man, who was new in town, was startled because he did not expect city people to care about one another, but he answered saying, "It's that the woman who came over last night seemed to really like me but she left this morning without making plans to see me again."

"I know what it's like. I thought it must be women that were troubling you because of that troubling look on your face. You ought to come to where I work tonight, because there are plenty of pretty ladies where I work."

"Where do you work?"

"A dance club."

"Oh no," said the man who was from a small town. "I don't mean that I want to pay a woman to take off her clothes."

That night as he sat in a booth by the wall, a tall voluptuous woman with red hair went and sat across from him. When she spoke her voice was tiny and girlish, and when he spoke back her eyes lit up, knowing a good man when she saw one. If he found her interest in him any consolation he did not show it, and continued to order drinks which cost seven dollars.

"Let me put that next one on my tab," she said, and adjusted her body in such a way that her breasts raised themselves parallel to the table. The man did not fail to notice this.

"Would you like to come home with me tonight?" he asked.

Growing suspicious, she said, "I thought you were a different sort of man, that's what Henry told me, and now you ask me the question everyone asks."

"I'm so ashamed," he responded sincerely. "I didn't mean it that way, but I don't like being alone, and you seem like a kind woman who would be a pleasure to spend good times with, even just talking."

She found this genuine enough and was touched that there was nothing of the brute in him; perhaps Henry was right. Even her so-called sisters, whom she hastily consulted in the back room, gave approving nods when they saw his modest eyes looking mainly at the fixtures.

The apartment was sticky because of the heat, and it wasn't long before they were lying in their underwear on his bed, and he was telling of how he had become a widower so young, which was a lie for he had never been married, or even in a real relationship twice. Since she had noticed him not noticing the dancers when she returned to the back room to get her regular clothes, she believed what he was saying; every word of it. There were simple ways some ladies had of telling a good guy from a bad, and her way was as stupid as any.

Quite soon she found herself giving him head and was trying her hardest because he seemed so patently not to be enjoying it. When he laid her he did so with great care and the air of a depressive, which made her trust him all the more.

It wasn't three weeks before they decided to live in an apartment together, which caused tension between the man and his roommate until a replacement was found.

Their life together was a gentle life of great delicacy and consideration, as they both felt sorry for the man, and he was also harbouring a great confusion at his sorrowful mood not being alleviated by the presence of this woman with the red hair.

Since in their hearts they both expected her to become pregnant, when she eventually did it was no great surprise. He merely stroked her arm as she lay across the base of the bed and cried about money. "I must go live with my sister," she told him. There was no part of her that was enthusiastic about living the life of a dancer with a young child. "Do you

122

want to come with me?" she asked.

He grew anxious at this request and began taking long strolls. Her sister lived in a small town with a husband and three kids, and the man, who was from out of town, had deliberately moved out of his town and had barely been in the city a year. When he thought about it now, the woman with the red hair hadn't been so difficult a catch; not so terribly hard to find a girl to spend good times with in a metropolis — he didn't know why he hadn't thought of it sooner. He declined and she ran away with her bags and her tears.

But it wasn't so easy the second time around to get a nice girl, and the man soon grew lonely. After two months he was forced to take in a roommate, but the only one he could find was smelly and young with a belly that hung out without discretion. This situation made the man even more lonesome than before, and one day at one o'clock in the afternoon he decided to visit the woman with the red hair. Walking past a fountain on his way to the train station, he passed a girl of late teenage years who was blonde and who he supposed would like the companionship of a man like him. Dragging her into the park he tore out two-thirds of her hair.

THE LITTLE OLD LADY
AND THE LITTLE OLD MAN

A little old man lived in a red-peaked house on the top of a hill in Dubrovnik. One day a woman came, and though at first he didn't recognize her, when she started speaking he certainly did.

"You're the woman I almost married," he said.

"Yes, that's right," she said. And they sat on the porch in two little chairs and looked out at the city over the hill.

"You look like an old woman now," he said.

"After you raped me my hair turned grey."

"Did it?"

"Within a week."

To this he nodded and sat back and said, "Would you like to go to the beach?"

She said fine, it made no difference to her, so the old man and the old woman got up and walked down the hill and around to the other side through a bramble of trees, and there was the beach leading into the sea, and the day was cold, and the old man and the old woman were warm.

She said, "It's beautiful, it really is. Look at how rocky it looks."

And he said, in a loud voice, "In fact, I think it's very still," and they stood there watching it, trying to understand who was right.

He turned to her after a moment and said, "You have any man in your life right now? Any children?"

And she said, "No one. I'm all alone and there's no one to take care of me, and I'm not lonely, but I'm alone all the same."

He turned to face the water and could see the little fishing village on the other side of the sea, and he said, "Sure you're lonely."

She didn't say a word.

"Let's walk along the shore," he said, but she did not want to.

He turned to her and said, "Why not?"

And she said, straight out, "I do *not* want to walk along the shore with you."

"Well, I'm going to walk along the shore without you then. You can just stand right here if you want."

And she said, "I do want."

So off he started to walk, and his back was frail but it had a few muscles that she could see through his shirt, and he walked proudly but with a bit of difficulty, and she stopped following him with her eyes and watched instead the waves get rockier.

She did not want to stand there by herself. It was silly. It was lonely. She had seen enough of the water. She watched him and watched his feet on the little stones, and she thought about how his view was constantly changing and how hers was always the same; the shore at the right turning that bit to the left, and the little pool on the left that had filled with clams.

And he was walking quite far off, and he thought angrily, "That's right, she didn't even come along." He wanted to go back and grab her by the arm, pull her with him, force her down the shore, but that thought went out of his mind as he turned and walked back towards her, where she was standing and staring, in the very same place, obstinate, mad.

He reached her face. There were their faces. There were their bodies. There were their toes.

She said quietly, "Oh, I don't know why I came. It seemed like a good day to do it. But now I'm tired, see, and I want to be getting on. You will take me to the railway station, won't you?"

And he said, "It'll be my pleasure."

But neither his horse nor his cart would start and neither would his tractor, and she said sadly then, as if not quite believing it, or as if simply playing wistful, "Well, then, I'll just walk."

"See you later then," he said hopefully. "Good of you to come by. I'm sorry you have no home."

The House at
the End of the Lane

Standing in the road at two in the morning the young man with the moonlight in his hair made a terrible fuss before his girlfriend.

"What sort of time? Who needs time?"

"*I* need time," the girlfriend said.

He shook his head and left, stopping at a distance beneath a lamppost. An old man was leaning against it, and tipping his hat he said with a grin, "The institution of long apprenticeships has no tendency to form young people to industry."

In the darkness the young man formed a tear. "I know," he said. "And it's obviously another man."

"Always is." But before the young man could begin his story the old man waved him away. "Come, let me show you something."

They walked for twenty minutes in silence through the

desolate streets of the town. No cars passed, the moon hung down, and the younger man thought calmly of his girlfriend's best friend Anne.

"No time is the right time for a second relationship," the old man said. He stopped before a house which stood, squat, at the end of a lane.

In the house it was warm and bare. They found, sitting on a fold-up chair, a red-haired woman named Stella, who was not only a fortune-teller but very vain. The old man said, "This is my friend. He's good-looking, isn't he? But he has got a long sad face, so I brought him here to cheer him up."

"Sit down," Stella said.

The young man sat down lightly. He had no reason to stand.

"I am a young married woman working to put my husband through school," the fortune-teller told him. "There is little time for study but every spare moment is spent reading and thinking. My life is somewhat lonely in the sense that it is difficult to find people among those around me who care to think and discuss past the ordinary concerns of earning and spending money and such. I am young, but my years have been filled with unusual experiences."

The young man looked at her face. It was weary and soft and not at all the face of a woman who was young. He said nothing, but neither did Stella or the man who had brought him, and so he said, "You're lying."

There was a little void, the old man coughed, a bit of shuffling, and the young man looked up and around. Stella got out of her chair and moved, then sat back down once more. The old man turned to face the window. Stella adjusted a button. A woman was walking by.

The old man said, "She's here to see you." The young man turned in his chair and saw the woman who had left him, now walking up the steps, now ringing the doorbell, now stepping inside to the tipped and welcoming hat of the older man.

"I'm sorry, John," she said. "I've thought things through."

The youngish man was displeased and unmoved.

"I want to be with you."

"No," he said, aware of his resistance. His insides felt like stones.

She asked him, "No?" embarrassed and afraid. Her eyes had filled with tears.

"I think no," the young man said. "My mother was once young like you. Then she had three children and now she lives alone." He left her through the open door.

"Sit down dear," Stella said.

"No!" cried the woman. "My heart is breaking and it's all your fault! You and all your talking!"

"You mustn't rush him," the old man said, pulling down his hat. "A young man needs some time to find his mind."

COWS AND BREAD

The man pushed the three cows out into the field. He was leaving them there to die.

He walked back to the house, closing the gate behind him. The thunderstorm was about to begin.

He saw his wife waiting for him, hands on her hips. As he approached he saw that she was smiling. When he got to the porch she frowned.

"I don't like what you're doing," she said, and went inside the house, shutting the door behind her. She would never forgive him for this.

The man stood on the porch and saw that the cows were now walking in circles, away from each other, and towards each other.

"Martha!" he called out, but she did not come. He wanted her to see this. "Martha!" he called again, but she still did not come. She had rejected him, just when he had created something beautiful for her.

The thunderclouds gathered and it started to rain. It

rained hard and cold, pelting down on everything. He ran into the house, leaving the door open. She was by the fireplace, knitting.

"Martha, come, it's about to start."

She did not look up. "I don't want to," she said, and continued knitting. There was a clap of thunder. "You're going to hurt those innocent animals."

"It'll be a wonderful spectacle!"

"I don't want to see it."

He sighed and went back outside, closing the door behind him. The animals were charred and dead in the field. He had missed the whole thing; the lightning shooting out of the sky, the three bolts striking the cows.

He walked back in and sat on a chair across from her.

"Well?" she said.

"I missed it," he said, and looked up at her face. After a couple of minutes of sitting he stood and walked into the kitchen. There he found two pieces of bread and some salty butter. He laid it on thick, then took it up to bed with him. He sat on the edge of the mattress and took a bite of bread, then put the pieces on the floor and went and stood at the pane.

"Would've been a beautiful sight," he said, pressing his nose against the glass. "Yup. A beautiful sight." He was dead sorry he had missed it.

THE MAN WITH THE HAT

The end of the day will come. How the man with the hat is afraid of this. How he clutches at his newspaper and walks through the streets with his legs clenched tight and thinks about it not at all.

Oh how nothing matters when the fact is: One day the lightning will come and the preachers won't be able to stop it and neither will the famous.

The man with the hat was sitting at a bar the other day, see, the best bar in the city with all the best folks to talk to, and he was going on about some "mail-order bride" he was considering shipping in from Honduras or maybe the Dominican Republic, he'd have to see. Then thinking to himself as the others wiped their mouths of their sloppy joe sandwiches:

"The tension of my audience will be transformed into an enormous burst of laughter, immediately drowned in applause. Frankly, I rather expect this will happen."

Then a voice from a typical boozer: "Tell us one of your stories, Joe."

"I just told you one of my fucking stories!" He rose with a bellow and shook his fist, peering around, looking for a fight.

"Get out ya bum."

So the man with the hat was walking through the streets again, looking up at the sky where the stars were shining and he felt like a miserable sack of shit. If a child could see him, in this state: to be picking fights when there were stars in the sky! And didn't he always forget the stars in the sky? What right had he? And didn't he know the meaning and beauty of the world, though he was only a lonely schmo? He was not going to be forgiven for this one, oh no!

And one block later: "I fear, concerning the manual labour of literary men. They ought to be released from every species of public or private responsibility. To them the grasshopper is a burden. I guard my moods as anxiously as a miser his money; for company, business, my own household chores, untune and disqualify me for writing. I think then the writer ought not to be married; ought not to have a family. I think the Roman Church with its celibate clergy and its monastic cells was right. If he must marry, perhaps he should be regarded happiest who has a shrew for a wife, a sharp-tongued notable dame who can and will assume the total economy of the house, and, having some sense that her philosopher is best in his study, suffers him not to intermeddle with her thrift."

Oh, his fucking thoughts! What difference were his fucking thoughts? That was it! For uselessness and shame and for crying out loud!

The man with the hat prostrated himself on the sidewalk; but what good was it? It was three in the morning and who would be coming by to beat him up or step on his back?

He crawled like a turtle into the middle of the road. Just run him over and make it quick, bud! The day would come but who the hell was he to live, talking about mail-order brides from Honduras or Barbados or the Dominican Fucking Republic. A beautiful girl never loved him, and his thoughts: Oh! His fucking thoughts were garbage. Let it end tonight!

Freeeeeeeeeeeeeeeeeeeeeeeeeep!

He scrambled off the road like a two-bit coward as the horn and the car blazed by him, and a man with a ruddy face leaned out the window, yelling, "You miserable mother-fucker get off the fucking road!"

What right had he to kill himself when there were stars in the sky, twinkling all innocent and not noticing him and noticing nothing. They were suspended so far and so beautifully and here he was putting himself on the road to get run over when he didn't even mean it.

The next day it was sunny and he awoke on a park bench with a bottle in his hand. He went at once to see his friend Jim.

Sitting on Jim's couch while Jim was in the next room stirring macaroni and cheese, just listening, the man with the hat hung his head low and told his story like a man ashamed. Jim interrupted, stomping into the room with the wooden spoon held up.

"You tell me the truth for once you godforsaken bastard."

Oh, if it wasn't the end of the world already! November thirteenth. A month and a half till the end of the world and everyone else had end-of-the-world plans but him. He didn't know what he would be doing.

The man with the hat started to sob and Jim went back to stir. Jim liked it real creamy. If it wasn't real creamy it wasn't worth shit. His friend had slept all night on a fucking park bench. Jim's girlfriend walked into the room in a man's shirt and looked so damn sexual the man with the hat moaned and covered his face with his hands.

"What's the story, boys?" her voice coming out like a six-year-old girl's, all turned-up at the end of every word. She pushed her soft hair behind her ear and leaned against the radiator with her leg showing to the hip. She smiled a big-lipped smile at the man with the hat, and in her head: "Madman, you are leaving me in the most beautiful mood of my life, in the phase of my love that is most real, most passionate, and most replete with suffering."

Jim, who could put his cock in her whenever he wanted and feel her luxurious tits morning noon and night, approached her with the wooden stick held up and suffered down upon her to leave them the fuck alone or else — and he made a sudden motion with the stick that sucked the breath right out of her, and she went to the shower, obedient and aroused.

"Come," said Jim, and the man with the hat went to the table, still covering his eyes.

"You've got to get a grip on your life," said Jim.

"What does that mean?"

"Oh good, well at least you can hear me. Then hear this: you're a bum. Don't you know that one day you're going to die. And then who's going to care? Marjorie?"

Marjorie was sunning herself with soap.

"Christ," said the man with the hat. "All right. I'll tell you the truth about it, as best I can."

"I don't want to hear the truth!" cried Jim. "What's the truth got to do with it? That's the problem with you, man, and that's the problem with your life. Forget about the truth. The truth's got nothing to do with your life. Are you a goddamned philosopher? Do you create anything? You walk around the streets thinking about yourself, thinking about the truth. Didn't you learn anything in school?"

"Like whad'ya mean?"

"Oh sheez."

They ate their macaroni and cheese in silence and Jim was so disgusted with the man with the hat that their lunch was unbearable, totally unbearable. They couldn't talk. They needed the outdoors, which was more vast and more forgiving.

"Come, let's go," said Jim, and the two men left and still the bitch was singing in the shower, making the man with the hat tingle with rage all over.

Outside they walked, and the man with the hat calmed down, for he had always walked, and Jim said, his voice contemplative and his skin absorbing the sun: "All right, see. All I'm getting at is this. You've got to think about what you want, then make a plan of how you're going to get it."

"A plan!" whined the man with the hat.

Jim said patiently, "You came to me, didn't you. Didn't you?"

They wandered into a park, and now the man with the hat was sitting on a bench and Jim was sitting in the grass before him and they were sharing a cigarette.

"Life," said Jim, looking at the trees, "is all about plans and action, plans and action. If you have no plan you can't take action. And if you're doing something and it's not in the plan, what do we call that? Messin' around."

Messin' around! So that's what he had been doing! The man with the hat was in agony. He rolled his face up to the sky.

"What I'm saying is making an impression on you," said Jim, encouraging. "What I'm saying is making sense. All right. Well, that's all you need to know. What's your plan? What do you want, boy!" Jim smacked him on the knee and looked at him hard.

The man with the hat was thinking, thinking.

Jim regarded him carefully and considered, "You ought, like me, to have studied church history for fifty years, to understand how all this hangs together."

"All right," said the man with the hat. "I've got a plan. I'll go home and I'll write, and for fifty fucking days I'll write, till the skin shows through my fingertips. Then I'll throw out every word that's a lie. Then I'll send it all in to the *Antigonish Review*. But a real beaut, word-processed and all."

Jim was thinking about Dolores.

"You're never going to make it," said Jim through his lips. "You haven't been listening to a word I've been saying."

That night the moon hung like a ball of sticky dough. The sky was a deep deep purple and children were walking about in Halloween costumes. Jim and the man were walking through the streets and the Halloween costumes sucked. The man with the hat noticed them all, but he was listening to Jim as Jim laid out the plan. Finally they arrived at Cedar Street.

"I've got to thank you man, truly. You've come through for me like no one has before." What did it matter that the plan was for a man with abilities — with thoughts not dreams? The man with the hat was through with truth.

Jim looked at him hard.

"You heard what I was telling you?"

"Oh yeah man, absolutely."

"And what are you going to do?"

"Go home, go home and write it down. It's only seven o'clock. I'm going to get a good night's sleep and begin anew at seven a.m."

A skeleton passed them by.

"And you're not scared?" asked Jim.

"Sure, sure, sure I'm not," said the man with the hat, shaking his head hard. He was so grateful and so moved. "I'm really going to do it."

Jim looked finally at the man and then walked off. The man with the hat rolled his eyes up to the sky and tears slipped down his face. He could see no stars, but he was happy. Oh, he was so happy. There was a heaving in his chest and it was not from the cigarette.

He had never had a plan, and it made everything clear. He knew what he had to do: follow the plan; and what he had to give up: anything that was not in the plan. Like standing on a street corner, looking at the sky.

He made his way home. He caught himself thinking, but his thought was not on the plan, was completely beside the plan, was even conspiring against it. He wasn't going to be a millionaire, but he would be busy with things to do. He had to make a resumé. First things first, Jim had said.

"I spent the winter in New York as usual, enjoying enormous success in everything I did." What had he to do with truth? It was a night in November. There were forty-two Novembers still to come.

"If I should write an honest diary, what should I say? Alas, that life has halfness, shallowness. I have almost completed thirty-nine years, and I have not yet adjusted my relation to my fellows on the planet, or to my own work. Always too young or too old, I do not justify myself; how can I satisfy others?"

Every plan fails. That's what the man had refused to tell him. Every single body's. But that, my friend, is precisely life's sorrow.

And now that he had it, he clutched it like a penny.

NOTES

In "Janis and Marcus," Marcus quotes from Saint-Simon's essay in *Voices of the Industrial Revolution* (Bowditch, John, and Clement Ramsland, eds. Ann Arbor: University of Michigan Press, 1968) when he says, "The philanthropists will continue . . ." and "In a word . . ."; Janis quotes from *A Mencken Chrestomathy* (New York: Knopf, 1962) when she says, "Some years ago . . ."

In "The Poet and the Novelist as Roommates," the poet says, "It has been so in politics, it has been so in religion, and it has been so in every other department of human thought." This is a quote from someplace; the author cannot remember from where.

In "The House at the End of the Lane," the old man quotes from Adam Smith's *Inquiry into the Nature and Causes of the Wealth of Nations* when he says, "The institution of . . ."; Stella quotes from Joseph Fletcher's *Situation Ethics* (Philadephia: Westminster Press, 1966) when she says, "I am a young married woman . . ."

In "The Man with the Hat," the man with the hat quotes from Salvador Dali's *Diary of a Genius* (London: Creation Books, 1994) when he says, "The tension of my audience . . ." and "I spent the winter in New York . . ."; he quotes from *The Heart of Emerson's Journals* (Mineola NY: Dover, 1958) when he says, "I fear, concerning the manual labour . . ." and "If I should write an honest diary . . ."; Jim's girlfriend speaks the words of George Sand in

143

Revelations: Diaries of Women (Moffat, Mary Jane, and Charlotte Painter, eds. New York: Random House, 1979) when she says, "Madman, you are leaving me . . ."; Jim speaks from *Conversations with Goethe* (London: George Bell and Sons, 1897) when he says, "You ought, like me, to have studied . . ."

"The Girl Who Was Blind All the Time," "The Girl Who Planted Flowers," and "The Poet and the Novelist as Roommates" first appeared in the good Sam Hiyate's *Blood & Aphorisms*. "The Giant" first appeared in *THIS Magazine*. "Eleanor" first appeared in *Toronto Life*. "What Changed" first appeared in *Taddle Creek*. "The Princess and the Plumber," "The Woman Who Lived in a Shoe," "The Littlest Dumpling," "The Favourite Monkey," "A Bench for Marianne and Todd," and "The Man from Out of Town" originally appeared in *McSweeney's*.

A NOTE ON THE AUTHOR

Sheila Heti was born in Toronto, Ontario, on Christmas Day, 1976, to a Jewish-Hungarian family. She moved to Montreal as a young woman to write for the theatre, then moved back. She ceased writing stories for this collection on May 1, 2000.

A NOTE ON THE TYPE

The text of this book is set in Bembo, modelled after a typeface cut in 1495 by Francesco Griffo for a book by scholar and priest Pietro Bembo. Griffo was an employee of the Venitian press Aldus Manutius, whose books helped to launch the Renaissance. Bembo is a fine typeface because of its well-proportioned letterforms, functional serifs, and lack of peculiarities; the italic is modelled on the handwriting of Renaissance scribe Giovanni Tagliente. Stanley Morison supervised the design of Bembo for the Monotype Corporation in 1929.

Titles are set in Joanna, designed by Eric Gill in 1930, based on type originally cut by sixteenth-century French publisher and letter cutter Robert Ganjon, a contemporary of Claude Garamond. Gill created the text face for the printing firm Hague & Gill, which he formed to give his idle son-in-law an occupation, and named the design for his daughter. It is, as Gill himself described it, "a book face free from all fancy business," with its small, straight serifs and a spare elegance that makes it notably attractive and distinguished.